COUNTRY DOCTOR

After years away, newly qualified Doctor Jane Ashford returns to her hometown in Essex to become a partner in her uncle's practice. Family and friends are delighted to see her again, including Steve Denny, whose crush on her has never faded. But then Jane meets local Doctor Philip Carson, both handsome and lonely; and when his touch kindles a desire that's almost painful in its intensity, she knows he's the right man for her. The problem is, Steve doesn't see it that way — and he intends to make it clear . . .

Books by Phyllis Mallett
in the Linford Romance Library:

LOVE IN PERIL
THE TURNING POINT
LOVE'S MASQUERADE
POOR LITTLE RICH GIRL
ISLE OF INTRIGUE
HOUSE OF FEAR
DEADLY INHERITANCE
THE HEART IS TORN
SINISTER ISLE OF LOVE
MISTRESS OF SEABROOK
HER SEARCHING HEART
TIDES OF LOVE
INTRIGUE IN ROME
DANGEROUS LOVE
IMPETUOUS NURSE
NURSE ON SKIS
PATIENT NURSE
MARRIED TO MEDICINE
DOCTOR'S DESTINY
EMERGENCY NURSE
DISTRICT NURSE
ROMANTIC DOCTOR

PHYLLIS MALLETT

COUNTRY
DOCTOR

Complete and Unabridged

LINFORD
Leicester

First published in Great Britain in 1969

First Linford Edition
published 2019

A catalogue record for this book is available
from the British Library.

ISBN 978–1–4448–4135–0

Published by
F. A. Thorpe (Publishing)
Anstey, Leicestershire

Set by Words & Graphics Ltd.
Anstey, Leicestershire
Printed and bound in Great Britain by
T. J. International Ltd., Padstow, Cornwall

This book is printed on acid-free paper

1

Jane Ashford drove the red sports car into the car park just off the market square in the little country town of Haylingford in Essex and looked around with gleaming brown eyes. This was the day she had been waiting for. She glanced at her watch and hopped out of the car, her long chestnut curls swishing about her tanned cheeks. The car park attendant hurried towards her, and Jane opened her bag and searched for a shilling.

'Hello, Mr Hector,' she greeted the man, and he paused to peer uncertainly at her.

'Why, it's Miss Jane Ashford!' he exclaimed, beaming.

'You're wrong,' Jane teased.

'Wrong? Why, I've known you ever since you were old enough to go to school. I'm not wrong.'

'I'm no longer Miss Ashford,' Jane teased.

'You're married?' He frowned. 'I haven't heard anything about that.'

'Not married!' Jane laughed musically. 'That will be the day. I'm thirty-two, almost, and I don't think I'll ever get married now. No, Mr Hector, I'm just teasing you. I'm Doctor Ashford now. This is my first day back in town, and I'm going into partnership with my Uncle John.'

'Doctor Ashford!' The old man smiled. 'I'm glad to hear you've qualified. If you prove to be half as good as your uncle, then we'll have no fears around here. But it doesn't seem possible. Why, only the other year you were hurrying to school off the bus. I remember it quite well.'

'It was a lot farther back than the other year,' Jane retorted. 'I was my uncle's receptionist for a few years, before he talked me into studying medicine. But now I'm qualified, and I'm here to help him in his practice.'

2

'Well, good luck to you, Doctor,' the old man said. 'I expect you'll be coming to see my wife if you're going to help your uncle. She's been ill for these past two years, and doesn't seem to be making any progress.'

'I'm sorry to hear that.' Jane nodded. 'I'll soon be getting into harness, and then I'll be making the rounds.' She gave him a shilling and turned to lock the car. She was going to call in on Uncle John before going home to her father's farm in the nearby village of Winchley.

Her steps were light as she walked along the hot pavements. July was gloriously hot this year, and she felt on top of the world as she gazed around the familiar streets. There was a different atmosphere here, or so it seemed, because she was back home. After qualifying, she had worked in a general hospital for two years, but now she was ready to take up a practice, and her uncle's long-awaited plans were about to take effect.

The surgery was in an old house in Rainbow Street, and Jane smiled to herself as she entered. It was a little past ten in the morning, and she found almost a dozen patients sitting in the waiting-room. They all gazed at her curiously, and some of them spoke, recognising her despite the long months she had been away, with only an occasional weekend spent at home. The receptionist came through, and she was a stranger to Jane, who was expecting to see old Miss Jameson, who had come out of retirement to take over from Jane after handing over to her some years previously.

'Yes?' The receptionist was young and efficient, blue eyed.

'I'm Jane Ashford. I'd like to see my uncle for a moment when he's free.'

'Oh! Yes, Doctor. Come through, won't you? I've been told to expect you.'

The curious glances of the patients became charged with interest, and Jane smiled as she followed the receptionist through to the private parts of the surgery.

'I'm Milly Andrews, Doctor,' the girl introduced herself. 'I hope you'll be happy here in the practice.'

'I'm sure I shall, Milly,' Jane replied. 'But what happened to Miss Jameson?'

'She died last week. She was in her seventies.'

'I'm sorry to hear that.' Jane's face clouded over. 'She was part of the fixtures here.'

'Yes, I can remember seeing her when I was brought here as a child, and she seemed very old then.'

'How do you like the job?' Jane studied the girl's face, liking what she saw. Milly Andrews was blonde and pretty, not more than eighteen, and Jane knew instinctively that her uncle had made a correct choice for his new receptionist.

'I like it very much. I'm only now beginning to settle in, but I wouldn't want to change the job for anything else.'

Jane nodded, recalling how she had felt when she filled the very same position. A door opened at her back, and she turned as a patient emerged from her uncle's surgery.

'You may go in now, Doctor,' Miss Andrews said, and Jane nodded.

Entering the surgery, Jane paused on the threshold to stare at her Uncle John. He was a tall, thin man of sixty-one, almost a twin of Jane's father Charles, although he was five years older. When he saw her he got quickly to his feet, smiling broadly as he came around the desk with outstretched hands.

'My dear Doctor Ashford!' he greeted jovially. 'At last you're here.'

Jane rushed into his embrace, and he kissed her warmly on the cheek. She blinked as emotion hit her, because this was a long-awaited moment and she knew how much he had been awaiting its arrival.

'Uncle John! This is the happiest moment of my life,' she said softly.

'I know exactly how you feel. I'm touched by the same emotion myself. It's been a long time, Jane, but the waiting has been worthwhile. You're here now, and I need you.'

'Are you very busy, then?'

'Not so much that as a wave of new patients from old Doctor Wyatt's practice. He died three weeks ago, and a new man has come in, but he's not popular, and we're getting the unhappy patients.'

'Doctor Wyatt dead?' Jane shook her head sadly. 'I've just heard about Miss Jameson. It was a shock not to see her here. She's been around for so long.'

'It was quite sudden. We buried her last Tuesday. I didn't get around to letting you know. It was your last week at the hospital, and I knew you'd be too busy finishing off there to be able to attend. The new receptionist is quite efficient for her age. I'm hoping she will decide to stay with us.'

'She seems quite happy with the job,' Jane declared. 'When do you want me to start, Uncle?'

'Before starting, let's have a little talk, but now isn't the time,' he replied with a smile. 'I'll be coming out to the farm this evening. We can talk then. Monday will do for your starting, but there are some details we'll need to discuss. You're going to live at the farm, aren't you?'

'Mother wants me to, and I suppose it will help, because any emergency calls from the outlying villages can come to me, and it will save you a long drive in the night.'

'I've been taking those long drives for a very long time,' he retorted, 'but, as you say, it will help. I'm not getting any younger, Jane. Now you'd better run along and get settled at home. I still have some patients to see, and then I have to go out on the rounds. Your surgery is on the top floor, and you may go up and look it over, if you like, but I'll show you around when I have more time.'

'Certainly, Uncle.' Jane nodded. 'I'll

go and take a look. But can I help you now? I'm ready to start work immediately.'

'I hope your enthusiasm will continue through the years,' he replied with a smile. 'But I'll manage today. It's going to be difficult for me to adjust to your presence, so let me have this last day to myself.'

'Are you regretting those plans you started so long ago?' she queried.

'No. Don't ever think that, Jane. I'm very happy indeed that you're here to help. I need that help, I don't mind telling you. I would have to take a partner soon, in any event, and I would rather you were here than some stranger.'

'That's all right then.' Jane moved to the door. 'I'd better not take up any more of your time, with patients waiting to see you. I'll take a look at my workshop, then go on home. I'll tell Mother to expect you this evening, shall I?'

'She's expecting me as it is,' came the

smooth reply. 'But wait one moment, Jane. I must tell you exactly what I think of your arrival. You've done extremely well so far, and I'm sure you'll be very happy in this practice. But I can't sometimes help wondering if medicine is for you. I sort of forced you into it, didn't I?'

'You did rather a lot of persuading,' Jane said with a smile. 'And I must thank you for being so forceful about it. I took the right step the day I started studying. I know that now, and I shall be eternally grateful for all your help and guidance, Uncle.'

'I've been wondering about it,' he said. 'It took you out of your environment, Jane, and you've never mentioned a boyfriend or shown any interest in one. I know your time has been taken up with studies and whatnot, but I can't help wondering if I didn't put too much upon your shoulders.'

'I assure you everything in my garden is lovely,' Jane told him.

'I'm glad. I played God in your life, Jane, starting you on this course, and that was a great thing to do. I've coloured your life, and if you don't like the patterns before you, then I've been very foolish.'

'Well, everything is all right, and I'm thankful you took me in hand.' Jane smiled. 'Now I'd better go or your patients will start complaining. See you this evening, Uncle.'

'I'm looking forward to it,' he retorted. He watched her to the door. 'Jane, there's one thing.'

'Yes?' She paused.

'Forget that Uncle business now. I'm John to you.'

'Certainly.' She smiled and nodded. 'Just a childish habit that's hard to break. See you this evening, John.'

There was a lightness in her breast as she departed, and Jane went up to the top floor, where she found her waiting-room and surgery neat and clean and waiting for her. She stared around the silent rooms, thinking of all the years

11

her uncle had been in practice here. She wondered about her own future, and there was just a twinge of wistfulness in her as she thought of the way she had left this town and gone away. She had left her friends, and made few new ones in her travels. Now she could not expect to come back and start again where she had left off years before. Time didn't stand still, and least of all for people.

Going down the stairs, she took her leave of Miss Andrews and walked out of the surgery. She was looking forward to the new patterns that would begin to take shape as she learned her way around the practice. When they were formed they would probably last for the rest of her life!

Driving the seven miles to Winchley, Jane swept through the village and on to her father's farm. She was smiling as she entered the driveway that led up to the big, comfortable farmhouse, and her heart was beating joyfully when she saw her mother emerging on to the front steps in anticipation.

'Mother!' Jane leaped out of the little car and hurried into her mother's welcoming arms. 'It's so good to be home.' She hugged and kissed her mother until both were breathless, and then she controlled her emotions and slipped her arm around her mother's slim shoulders.

Mrs Ashford was small against Jane, but they had the same brown eyes and gentle features. Ellen Ashford didn't look all of her fifty-four years, and her happiness now at having her only child back home with her took even more time off her face.

'Jane, I've been watching the road for hours! I'm so happy you've come back home.'

'Not as happy as I am to be here,' Jane retorted. 'Let me get my cases out of the car, and then we'll talk while I unpack.'

It was a joyous time for Jane as she unpacked her clothes and put them away in her own room. Homecoming was always a pleasant affair, but until now there had always been the knowledge that she would have to go away again later. Now that niggling thought was absent from the back of her mind, and her happiness knew no bounds. She questioned her mother closely about the affairs of those people she knew, and Mrs Ashford chattered on eagerly.

'Roger Keeble broke off his engagement with that girl he planned to marry. I can't think of her name. You thought a lot of Roger at one time, didn't you, Jane?'

'You know I did, Mother.' Jane smiled thinly as she recalled. 'But he had a roving eye, and I gave him his choice. It seems he can't keep a girlfriend at all. But he's not the marrying kind. I feel sorry for any girl who has to take him in hand.'

'Dorothy Beck has set herself up with a hairdressing salon in Bridge Street. You'll have to pop in and see her. I told her you were coming home for good, and she was very interested.' Mrs Ashford sat down on the bed and watched Jane's face. 'You'll find a lot of your old friends around, and it's surprising the number who haven't married.'

'Perhaps there's something in the water around here.' Jane said with a smile. 'But I shan't get much time to go gallivanting as I did in the old days. I'm a responsible member of the community now.'

'You're still young, Jane, and you ought to have some fun while you still can.'

'That sounds like good, motherly advice.' Jane sat down beside her mother and took her hands. 'I'm very happy the way things are now, mother, so don't start worrying about my welfare.'

'You took on a great deal when you decided to follow in John's footsteps. Sometimes I wonder if it wasn't too much for you, or that John and your father expected too much. If you had been a boy it would have been different.'

'My name would probably have been James, I expect,' Jane retorted with a laugh. 'Mother, don't start having second thoughts at this late stage. Would you rather I forgot the whole thing now, after the worst part of it is over? I could open up a hairdressing salon in opposition to Dorothy Beck.'

'No, dear, and you mustn't heed my doubts. It's just that I find it hard to see you as a qualified doctor. My own little girl has grown up and can stand on her own two feet without any help from me. Perhaps it's that I'm afraid to admit it because then I have to acknowledge that I'm getting old.'

'Mother, are you all right?' Jane stared into her mother's eyes, looking for deep worry. 'Or is this a phase that comes to all mothers at some time in their lives? Have you been getting out and about enough?'

'Your father and I lead a very full life, as you know. I'm quite happy with my lot, Jane. But I made a free choice. You were persuaded to take up medicine, and although I agreed with it at the time I'm not so sure now.'

'I took it up because that was what Fate intended for me to do,' Jane said. 'Anyway, I'm quite happy with my lot. I can't wait until Monday to get started.'

'Hello, up there!' A voice called strongly from the hall, and Jane sprang to her feet.

'It's Father!' she cried, and dashed from the room. She met her father on the wide landing, and he swept her off her feet as he hugged and kissed her.

'Jane, it's wonderful to have you home again. This house has been a dreadful place without you. And apart from that, it will be very handy with a doctor in the house.' He grinned at her, a tall, thin, cheerful man. 'You're going to live here with us, aren't you? John said something about asking you to stay at his place in town.'

'I'll stay here, if I may,' she retorted.

'I wouldn't feel comfortable anywhere else.'

'That's good.' Charles Ashford looked up at his wife, now standing in the doorway of Jane's room, and he nodded in relief. 'Did you hear that, Ellen? She won't be staying anywhere else.'

'I would have been distressed had she decided on anything else,' Mrs Ashford said happily. 'We haven't seen much of her in the past few years. I want to see something of her before she finds a man and decides to get married.'

'I have the feeling that event may never take place,' Jane told them as her mother joined her and started down the stairs. 'Can you imagine me as a dried-up old spinster doctor in another twenty years?'

'Don't talk about the future like that,' her mother retorted. 'Time will pass quite fast enough without you bringing it closer.'

'I'm beginning to realise that for myself,' Jane said, nodding. 'It is a true saying that this is a very short life. I've lived almost half mine already, and I haven't even settled down in what must become my life's work.'

'Steady on, you two,' Charles Ashford said firmly. 'What is this morbidness? That's not the way to look around you. Live each day as it comes, that's my motto. And listen to this. I thought I'd arrange a welcome-home party for you, Jane. I saw Roger Keeble at the cattle market this morning, and told him you were coming home today. I asked him if he would round up some of your old friends, if they were available, and get them to come here this evening. He promised he would, so you and Mother had better start organising things. You'll likely have a large gathering on your hands.'

'Father!' Jane's voice trilled with happiness. 'You really are the limit.' She turned to face her mother. 'What about it? Can we do something at such short notice?'

'Let's try.' Mrs Ashford forgot her

doubts and took Jane's arm. 'Come into the kitchen and say hello to Mrs Gartside, and we'll spring the news on her. Father can take the blame if she doesn't take kindly to the idea.'

Jane nodded, pleased with the prospect, and after she had spoken with the cook she left her mother to make the arrangements for the evening. Her father was in his study, and Jane stood in the hall and looked around at the familiar furnishings. This was home. It was wonderful to be back. There was no place like home! The saying had become trite through common usage, but it still had a magic that no amount of familiarity could mar.

The doorbell rang shrilly behind her, and Jane was momentarily startled. She turned quickly in answer, and found a tall, strange man standing on the step.

'Good morning!' Jane said easily. He had the look of a travelling salesman about him, being in his early thirties, with a smoothness about him that spoke volumes.

'Good morning,' he responded. 'I'm sorry to trouble you, but I noticed the telephone wires leading here from the road, and I wonder if I might use your instrument? My car has broken down about a mile from here, and I'm a doctor on my country round.'

'Certainly, Doctor. Please do come in.' Jane smiled as she stepped back and opened the door. 'A breakdown is one of the worst things that can happen to a doctor.'

'Thank you!' He smiled, his blue eyes upon her face. 'I'm Doctor Carson, from Haylingford.'

Jane showed him the telephone standing in the hall, and moved away while he used the instrument. Her mother appeared from the kitchen and came towards her, and Jane told her quietly what was happening. They listened to Doctor Carson ringing a garage, and then he put down the receiver. His face was grim as he turned towards them.

'Thank you so much,' he said.

'There'll be someone out to take a look at the car very shortly. What do I owe you for the call?'

'Nothing, Doctor!' Mrs Ashford went forward before Jane could speak. 'So glad we could be of help. I'm Mrs Ashford, and this is my daughter Jane.'

'Can I drive you anywhere, Doctor?' Jane demanded before her mother could say more. 'I know how important time is to a man in your profession.'

'I couldn't put you to that trouble,' he replied. 'But you are very kind.'

'I heard you say your car is about a mile along the road. You can't walk all that way back to it. My car is outside. It won't be any trouble for me.'

'Well, thank you. I shall be heavily in your debt.' There was a seriousness about him, although he smiled, and Jane moved to the door, and opened it before looking at her mother.

'I won't be long, Mother,' she said. 'This is the least I can do.'

'Of course, dear.' Mrs Ashford came to the door as they departed.

Doctor Carson paused in the doorway. He had blond hair that curled behind his ears. His blue eyes were filled with light as he thanked Mrs Ashford again.

'I'll do anything for the medical profession,' she said, glancing at Jane. 'My brother-in-law is a doctor, and so is my daughter.'

Carson looked at Jane with a startled expression on his face. She smiled at sight of it, but for some obscure reason she wished her mother hadn't mentioned the fact. She had the feeling this was the doctor who had taken over Doctor Wyatt's practice in Haylingford and was proving most unpopular.

'Ashford,' he said half to himself. 'Of course! I ought to have recognised the name. Doctor John Ashford, and I heard a niece was coming to share his practice. This is most interesting.'

Jane didn't think so as she led him towards her car. He had trouble squeezing himself into the bucket seat at her side, and Jane felt awkward as she waited for him to close the door. She started the car, feeling all fingers and thumbs, and was aware that he watched her keenly as she concentrated upon her driving. He directed her to the spot where he had left his car, and they soon reached it.

'I'll wait with you in case they can't fix your car immediately,' Jane offered as she pulled on to the verge.

'I can't impose upon you just because we are in the same profession,' he retorted.

'Perhaps you'll be able to do the same for me sometime in the future,' Jane pointed out.

'That's possible, but I don't want to be any trouble to you,' he persisted.

'It's no trouble at all. I have nothing else to do. I arrived home today, and I don't take up my duties until Monday.'

'All right.' He gave in a trifle ungraciously, and Jane took the trouble to study him as they sat waiting for the breakdown van to show up. They chatted about their profession, and he asked some questions about her training and the people she knew. It transpired they had mutual friends, but he had known those people before she. He gave her the impression that he didn't want to be friendly, and she imagined it was because some of his patients were coming into her uncle's practice. But he was appreciative of the way she was helping him. Jane was thoughtful after she left him later, with his car in working order. Something about him intrigued her . . .

2

Getting back home in time for lunch, Jane had no chance of considering Doctor Carson. She had been struck by an odd note in his manner. It had seemed to her that he was sad about something, but that might have been her impressions getting mixed up. He knew a lot of his patients were going to the Ashford practice, and perhaps he hadn't liked it. That would have been natural, she supposed, but she was more concerned why he wasn't popular. But she didn't get the chance to think it out. There was the evening to prepare for. During the afternoon various friends kept ringing up to say they'd got the message and would be coming to the farm for the evening. Jane began to get excited as the time drew nearer. Some of her friends she hadn't seen for years.

At seven she answered the first ring at the doorbell to find Roger Keeble standing there. He was thirty-five, tall, dark, and handsome as ever, and he took Jane's hand in a powerful grip as he crossed the threshold.

'Am I the first?' he demanded.

'Yes,' she replied. 'Does it matter?'

'I like being first,' he retorted. 'How are you, Jane? I'm very happy to see you back again. Perhaps we can get together sometime to talk about the past.'

'I don't have much to talk about in that respect,' she replied with a smile. 'I'm sure you wouldn't want to know about lectures and studies.'

'I was talking about our past,' he returned. 'We were good friends, Jane.'

'We'll have to see how the practice accepts me,' she said. 'Come and have a drink.'

Jane took him into the large lounge, where her mother and father were seated, and soon Roger was talking about farming with her father, although he kept his eyes upon Jane. When the doorbell rang again, Jane hurried in answer, and found her uncle coming in.

'John, I'm afraid we shan't get much time for talking this evening,' she apologised as she took his hat. 'Father arranged for some of my friends to call this evening as a sort of welcome-home party. But come in. You'll know everyone, no doubt.'

'It sounds very cosy,' he replied as they walked along the carpeted hall.

'Before we go in,' Jane said, touching his arm. She mentioned her meeting with Doctor Carson. 'Have you ever met him, John?'

'I've seen him. He doesn't strike me as being a friendly sort. I have heard he's preoccupied about something. His patients all complain that he's not at all like Doctor Wyatt was.'

'Well, of course, he's a much younger man, and a stranger,' Jane pointed out. 'One has to get used to a doctor before complaining that he doesn't fill the bill as well as a predecessor. Did they give him a chance?'

'Some of them did. But the chief complaint was by the women. Doctor Carson isn't married, and they don't like a single doctor examining them. Women run the households these days, you know, and if the wife says she wants to change her doctor then the husbands don't object.'

'I see.' Clare pictured Doctor Carson's lean face, and a frown showed between her eyes. Then the doorbell rang and she was jerked from her thoughts. 'Go in, John,' she said. 'I'll be busy here for some time, I expect. But we'll have a chat before you decide to call it a day.'

He nodded and left her, and Jane went back to the door. When she opened it she found two girls on the step, and they came forward to greet her cheerfully.

'Dorothy Beck, I haven't seen you in a long time,' Jane exclaimed as she took the hands of the nearer of the two.

'Mother was telling me about your hairdressing business. I shall have to visit you soon.'

'I shall be glad to see you, Jane,' the girl replied, smiling. She was tall and slim and blonde, and a few years younger than Jane. 'But I hope you won't expect me to call you in because of it. I hope we never meet professionally, from your point of view, of course.'

'You look the picture of health, Dot,' Jane retorted, her eyes taking in the good figure of her friend. Then she looked at the second girl, who was smiling cheerfully. 'Kay Lanham! Good Lord, I do believe I would have passed you had we met in the street. It's been such a long time since I last saw you.'

'Jane!' the girl exclaimed. 'I would have known you anywhere.'

'Is that good?' Jane demanded, and they all laughed. 'But come on in. I don't know who is coming this evening. Roger is here already.'

'Roger Keeble?' Dorothy Beck paused

on the threshold. 'Then I'd better go, Jane.'

'Oh?' Jane stared at the girl. 'Have you had some trouble with Roger?'

'He came to me on the rebound,' Dorothy said primly. 'Did you know he was engaged to be married?' She lowered her voice as she glanced towards the door of the lounge. 'It was some girl he met away somewhere. They went together for months, but it was suddenly broken off. But you know what Roger is like. You went around with him for years.'

'Only as friends,' Jane pointed out quickly. 'Roger never appealed to me in that way. And I wouldn't take him seriously because he was always turning aside after some other girl.'

'His habit has never changed,' Dorothy retorted. 'I took pity on him a month or so ago, but he suddenly dropped me again without any reason given.'

'Well, come in now and show him that you don't care,' Jane said, taking the girl's arm. She closed the door as they entered, and leaned her back against it. 'What about you, Kay? Is there a man in your life, or are we all suffering from the same strange malady?'

'I have a boyfriend, but I'm not very keen on him,' Kay Lanham admitted. She was a petite brunette, with liquid brown eyes. 'I hope you'll come and visit me when you get time, Jane. I run the dress shop in the High Street.'

'Really? I'll certainly come and see you. I'm not very dress conscious, I warn you, but perhaps you'll be able to instil some responsibility into me. Perhaps you'll know how a country doctor ought to dress.'

'Certainly not in tweeds and long dresses,' Dorothy Beck said with a laugh. 'By the way, I saw Steve Denny this afternoon and mentioned that your friends were gathering here this evening. He said he might call in. Did he ring you?'

'No.' Jane shook her head, conjuring

up a picture of Steve. He had always been sweet on her in the past, but had never tried to do anything about it. 'What's he doing these days?'

'Working in his father's building firm,' Kay said. 'I've seen him around quite a lot.'

'Well, come and join the throng and we'll see what the evening brings forth,' Jane told them. 'I don't suppose we'll get much chance to do any chatting this evening, but we'll get together again very soon, girls.'

'I shall look forward to it,' Dorothy told her.

Jane led the way into the lounge, and the menfolk got to their feet at their entrance. Jane saw Roger's eyes shine when he saw her companions, and she shook her head regretfully. Roger would have been a very good friend if his unfortunate weakness hadn't taken him along devious paths. But she felt that he would never settle down. Perhaps he, too, was touched by that intangible finger which selected those in life to remain unmarried.

They chatted together about the years when they had seen little of each other, and they were all interested in Jane's life. She found herself the centre of attraction, and a sense of well being came to her as she warmed to them. These were all part of her youthful days, part of the unrecallable past. The years between had flown by, or so it seemed, and it was pleasant to recall those earlier times when they had been standing on the threshold of life with their choices for the future still before them.

The doorbell rang again and Jane hurried in answer. She found Steve Denny waiting on the step, and he grinned at her and held out a small, fleshy hand as she invited him in.

'Jane, I am glad to see you again,' he said. 'Why the devil have you been away for so long?'

'All in the line of duty,' she replied, shaking hands with him. 'How have you been keeping, Steve?'

'Fine. And I've been looking for you to return to us ever since I heard that you would be joining your uncle's practice,' he said. 'It's good to see you, Jane.'

'Are you coming in?' As she remembered him, he was rather shy, she thought.

'Yes.' He crossed the threshold. 'It's a long time since I was here. I hope it won't be as long before I'm asked again, Jane.'

'Now that I'm back in circulation around here we should be seeing a lot of one another,' she agreed. 'You're working in your father's business, aren't you, Steve?'

'That's right.' He nodded. 'Who else is here?'

'Roger Keeble, and Dorothy Beck and Kay Lanham. You know them all, don't you?'

He nodded. Jane led the way to the lounge, and she had the feeling that the years had changed Steve. He was a year or two younger than she, and her recollections of him were of a small, nervous type of boy who had been bullied at school. But now he was thick-set and strong, and she couldn't imagine anyone trying to push him around. There was an air about him that told her he would stand no nonsense from anyone, and when they entered the lounge she was pleased to see that he was quite sure of himself. He greeted everyone in friendly fashion, and sat down beside Dorothy. Jane gave him a drink and the conversation went on in general terms.

By the end of the evening Jane was enjoying the old familiarity she had held with these friends, and they were more like their old selves. She could now see the children out of which these men and women had grown, and it was uncanny recalling the past and remembering them as they had been. But eventually they decided to leave, and Steve offered to drive the two girls back to town. Roger lingered at the door after the others had gone, and he took

Jane's hands as he stared into her face. The evening was still bright, despite the growing lateness of the hour, and Roger could not help trying to exert his personality.

'Jane, it's been wonderful seeing you again. I hope we'll meet again quite soon.'

'You must be pretty busy with that large farm of yours,' she retorted, knowing how to handle him. 'I know my father doesn't get much time to himself.'

'But I can always make time for you,' he countered, pulling her towards him.

'Then give me a ring sometime,' she said, bracing herself. 'I don't know yet what free time I shall have, but I'll always be happy to see you, Roger.'

'Good.' He nodded, quite sure of himself. 'I've wasted a lot of time, Jane. I've been a fool most of my life, but I have hopes that I'll change now.'

'I hope you will, for your sake,' she told him with a smile. 'Now, good night, Roger.'

'Good night.' He turned away reluctantly, and Jane watched him for a moment or two as he went towards his large car. When he turned to glance back at her, she lifted a hand, and then went into the house and closed the door. She sighed as she went into the lounge.

'Well?' her father demanded. 'Did I do the right thing in passing on the word this morning?'

'Yes, Father,' she said. 'It was nice seeing them all again. Now they know I'm back, the word will soon get around. I expect there will be a lot of callers at the surgery who will just want to take a look at me.'

'Perhaps we can have a talk now, Jane,' John said, smiling. 'I shall be on my way to bed very shortly.'

'Certainly. I'm sorry you had to wait all evening before getting down to business. I looked around my surgery before I left this morning, and you've certainly spared no pains or expense to get everything just right.'

'I'm glad you liked it.' He was pleased. 'I told them not to spare anything. You'll be spending quite a lot of your time in those rooms, Jane, so you want the atmosphere to be just right. But let's get down to cases. I usually have Wednesday nights off. You can pick whichever night you want. Give it some thought. You don't have to rush into it. I suggest we take it in turns to handle the surgery in the mornings, either on a daily or a weekly basis, and we'll take turns with evening surgery. On Monday you can have the surgery and I'll do the rounds. I'll have Monday evening in the surgery. On Tuesday you can do the rounds in the morning while I have the surgery, and you can take evening surgery; and so on. How does that strike you?'

'Very workable,' Jane replied. 'And what about clinics and the like?'

'I'm glad you brought that up.' He smiled. 'I shall be happy to hand some of that work over to you, and perhaps you can hold them more often than I've been in a habit of doing. But get together with the District Nurse on that. She has been doing a great deal in those areas herself.'

Jane felt her enthusiasm mounting as they talked, and her parents sat listening, filled with a new respect for her as they heard of some of the things she would be handling. Jane was content now. She had worked towards this end for a great many years, and at times it had seemed to her that all the planning would come to naught, but here she was back where she started out, but with the necessary qualifications. She had great cause to be happy.

Later, in the sanctuary of her room, she lay in bed thinking over the past, and what her life might be in future. Her feet were firmly planted upon the threshold of success, and the degree of it would come from the extent of her own endeavours. She vowed that nothing would come between her duty and herself. She would spare no pains to do the very best she could in any situation or circumstance. Then she closed her eyes and slipped easily into sleep.

The next day started fairly late, for she overslept and her mother wouldn't call her. It was ten-thirty when Jane descended the stairs to find a glorious summer day awaiting her. She took a light breakfast, and sought out her mother, who was habitually an early riser.

'What are you going to do today, Jane?' Mrs Ashford demanded. 'No doubt you'll want to get out to look around the old familiar places. It's the sort of thing I would do were I in your shoes.'

'I do have some sort of a plan in the back of my mind,' Jane admitted. 'I think I'll walk around the village, and later I'll drive around the other areas that I shall have to cover as a doctor. John was telling me that as well as Winchley we have patients in Brookby, Cossett and Swanstoft. That means quite a lot of driving around.'

'Are you sure in your own mind that this is exactly what you want, Jane?'

'How do you mean?'

'You're burying yourself in the country. Wouldn't you have been far happier working in a hospital, or with a practice in one of the cities?'

'No. I'm quite happy where I am. I'm a rustic at heart, and there is no doubt about that. The big cities are all right, but they don't appeal to me. Don't worry about me, Mother. I'm very happy with the way things are.'

'I'm so glad, Jane. I've been worried for years now, because you've been working so hard, and I was afraid that when this time came you would discover that you don't like the position. But you seem very happy.' She smiled and took Jane's hand. 'I'm very proud of you, my dear. John said on the day you were born that he wished you had been a boy. In those days it was almost unheard of for a woman to become a doctor. But times have changed, and I expect John's cup is running over right now.'

'I'm so happy that everyone else is happy,' Jane said with a smile.

'You've always been an unselfish girl. You're not putting on a happy face just because this is what everyone wants you to do, are you?'

'No.' Jane shook her head and smiled. 'I wouldn't do that, Mother, not even for John.'

'Then no more need be said. I hope everything will work out exactly as you want it to, Jane.'

Jane kissed her mother's cheek. 'It's wonderful being back home again,' she remarked. 'I'm going out now, for a walk. What time is lunch?'

'About twelve-thirty, dear. I won't suggest accompanying you because it's always nicer to take that first walk alone.'

'You're the most understanding mother!' Jane retorted. 'See you when I get back.'

She set out immediately, controlling an urge to run along the road, such was her joy. She walked the half-mile to the village, and stared around as if she had never seen it before as she strolled the narrow streets. She could remember the countless times she had run around here as a girl. Now she was a grown woman with a responsible job and a great duty towards the community. It gave her a nice feeling inside to know that she had special skills, and the great job of healing lay at her fingertips.

Of course, she didn't expect any earth-shattering diseases to come her way, no epidemics of mortal plagues. No doubt she would get a little tired of the run of general complaints, the colds and sicknesses attendant upon normal, everyday living, but they would not be merely cases, but people, human beings in misery who wanted and needed the relief which she would be able to give. Then there would be the women having their families. She would take a great interest in that side of the job. Her enthusiasm flared as she walked, and her steps quickened in sympathy with her teeming mind. She wished it were Monday morning so she could make a start.

A car pulled into the kerb as she paused near the village post office. Steve Denny alighted, a smile on his fleshy face. He came towards her eagerly, dressed smartly in grey flannels and sports jacket.

'Jane, I could hardly believe my luck when I spotted you. I was on my way to call on you. I ought to have asked last night, but didn't really get the chance. What about coming out with me this evening?'

'Steve, it's nice of you to ask.' Jane smiled as she nodded. 'I haven't made any arrangements, and it is my last evening before I take up my duties in the practice. I'd like to go out with you. It's been such a long time since we walked together.'

'I'll walk with you now,' he offered. 'I'm not going anywhere special. But tell me, Jane, did Roger ask you last night to go out with him?'

'He didn't. Roger knows me too well to ask, I expect.'

'He'll never change, will he? He telephoned me this morning to find out what my intentions were, and he said you had arranged to see him again. So he's going to pay you some more attention now you're back.'

'I expect I'll find I have some pretty strong views on that,' she said, smiling despite the tension in her voice. 'I don't think Roger will bother, though, after what we've been to each other and the way we parted.'

'I'm glad to hear that. He's not good enough for you, Jane.' Steve fell into step beside her, leaving his car at the kerb. Jane paused, her eyes studying his intent face.

'Hadn't you better lock it, Steve?' she demanded.

'Of course! That just shows, doesn't it? You turn my thoughts upside down, Jane.'

'You've changed,' she remarked when they walked on. 'I can remember when

46

you were the shyest boy I knew.'

'I've grown up some since then.' He laughed as he looked into her brown eyes. 'But no one could be shy around you, Jane. I knew that last night. We were always good friends in the past, weren't we?'

'Of course.' She nodded vehemently. 'I've always liked you, Steve. I've often thought about you while I was away.'

'That's glad tidings, anyway,' he remarked. 'But I wouldn't want to see you getting interested in Roger again, Jane. He'd break your heart without a second thought for you.'

'You forget that I know Roger better than most,' she said wisely. 'I saw through him a long time ago, and he hasn't the power to attract me again. I like him very much. He's always been a special friend, but I do know this much, Steve. If he was the last man alive, I wouldn't fall for him. There's nothing wrong with him as far as it goes. It's just that he and I are too far apart in everything. I value his friendship, and he knows it. But we could never be anything more than friends.'

'The more you say this morning the better I like it,' he retorted. 'I've been waiting for you to come back, Jane. I've known for some time now that you were coming back and that there was no man in your life. I have a good position in my father's firm, and no doubt I'll take over the business in the future. I want to tell you that you're a very special girl in my eyes, Jane. Bear it in mind, will you?'

She nodded, although she was a little surprised by the tension in his tones. She hadn't known he was capable of such depths, and she looked at him with new understanding as they continued to stroll. He certainly had grown up, and he was just the sort of man a woman doctor ought to marry. The thought startled her, and she was silent for some time, turning over in her mind the fresh ideas that came from this meeting with Steve. Somewhere deep inside her there was a desire that came to life of its own volition. She was a normal girl despite the dedication she felt for her work. Her intensive studying had left little time for natural pastimes and activities, and it came to her suddenly, surprisingly, that she had paid little or no attention to romance or marriage. They didn't enter into her calculations or the scheme of things, but she knew instinctively that she was making a mistake. Marriage was something that ought to be allowed for!

She smiled slowly as she considered the subject, but what was surprising in her summing up, as she wondered what kind of a man would attract her, was the fact that Steve didn't ring the bell in her mind, and neither did Roger. A stranger's face appeared from nowhere to confront her, and it belonged to Doctor Carson.

3

When she left Steve in the village to walk back to the farm, Jane felt as if she were in another world. In her mind there was a picture of Doctor Carson, and the more she wondered about him the deeper grew her uneasiness. Meeting her friends the evening before had put a stop to the feelings that had started growing after meeting Doctor Carson that morning, but now he was in her mind with a vengeance and pushing down tenacious roots.

She was concerned because he was losing patients, and there had seemed to be an aloofness about him which instantly attracted her. He was not married! She recalled what John had told her about Doctor Carson. But why was he so unpopular with the patients in the practice he had taken over? Jane tried to shake herself from the course her mind seemed to have chosen, but the more she tried the firmer the thoughts remained.

After lunch she went out in her car, driving around the villages she would have to visit during her rounds as a doctor. She knew them all, of course, but it was years since she had been in any of them. Now it was like a pilgrimage, looking at the half-forgotten sights and bringing back all the details that had slipped her mind. Yet she was aware that somewhere in the back of her thoughts there was a disturbing influence.

After visiting the villages, she drove on to town, and entered Haylingford at about four. She passed John's house, but did not stop, and before she knew where she was she had stopped near the house that had belonged to old Doctor Wyatt. It was a large, grey-stone building with blank-looking windows and a general air of neglect. Old Doctor Wyatt hadn't concerned himself with the upkeep of the house, and it seemed that his successor was similarly minded. To Jane it was another pointer to Doctor Carson's character, and she found she was forming a picture of his personality from the few pointers so far obtained.

She didn't stop to consider why she was taking an interest in this stranger. Perhaps it was because they were in the same profession! But, at any rate, she was concerned about him because he was losing patients. Every doctor started out after qualification with the highest ideals. But something had happened to Doctor Carson to change him. It was as if he didn't care that his practice was falling to pieces.

Jane was so lost in thought over the subject that she didn't notice the door of the house opening. Doctor Carson was opening the gate before she realised that he was before her, and her heart seemed to miss a beat when he came to the car. The windows were down, and he bent to peer into the little car at her. His blue eyes were very keen and alert as he stared at her. Jane felt her throat constrict until the sides seemed to be touching, and guilt flashed through her.

'Good afternoon, Doctor Ashford,' he greeted her in expressionless tones. 'I couldn't mistake the car after yesterday's ride in it. Were you just sightseeing, or were you contemplating a social visit? There aren't many of us in the town, and your practice has two-thirds of the total medical strength.'

'Good afternoon, Doctor Carson,' she replied, afraid that her face would show her inward feelings. 'I didn't mean to be rude, but I'm a nostalgic person deep inside, and learning yesterday of Doctor Wyatt's death was a shock. I knew him quite well, and after meeting you yesterday I thought I'd come by and look into the past, as it were. Just sitting here and thinking of the old doctor is a way of paying my respects to his memory.' She paused. 'I hope you won't think me too mixed up.'

'Not at all. I was pleased to see you, come to that. Sunday is always a dreadful day for me. I'd rather be working, and I sometimes sit by the phone hoping it will ring.'

'Really?' Jane frowned. 'Haven't you made any friends in town since you've been here?'

'No.' He shook his head. 'I usually keep myself to myself. I don't really feel that I belong here. You don't know it yet, but as soon as you start your duties you're going to find that a lot of Doctor Wyatt's practice is coming to you.'

'I'm sorry to hear that. What's the reason?' Jane was interested for the fact alone. She couldn't see any serious defects in his personality. His bedside manner would be quite correct, and the fact that he was single wouldn't count at all against him. Patients didn't care who the doctor was when they really needed one.

'Would you care to come into the house?' he demanded. 'Are you familiar with it?'

'It's been years since I was last inside,' Jane said. Her heart was pounding for some unaccountable reason. 'Yes, I would like to see inside it again. But I'm not disturbing you in any way, am I?'

'Certainly not. I've got to the stage where I've been watching the flies crawling up the windows. Do come in. Perhaps I can make some tea. My cleaning woman doesn't come in on Sundays, and I take care of the place myself, but all the work is done now, and I'm just sitting around waiting for tomorrow to dawn.'

'But that's dreadful!' Jane got out of the car and locked it. 'If I had known, Doctor, I would have asked you over to the farm for the day.'

'Would you?' He stared at her with bright blue eyes, and Jane felt her heart miss a beat. He was lonely, and seemed to be in the depths of despair. But why was he so lonely? Her own great happiness at being home and feeling on top of the world seemed to turn to guilt as she imagined what his life must be, living for nothing but duty. It must be intolerable! She caught her breath as she followed him into the house, for there was an atmosphere of hopelessness which hurt her throat.

'We're both doctors, and as such we should get together,' she declared. 'Why haven't you approached my uncle before now?'

'I don't think it's up to me to make the first move,' he retorted, closing the door at her back. 'I'm the stranger here. I've seen your uncle, and he does look rather formidable. Probably he wouldn't thank me for barging in on him.'

'But Uncle John is one of the best,' Jane told him eagerly. She looked around the hall, which ran through to the back of the house. 'This place hasn't changed much, from what I remember. Doctor Wyatt lived here for more years than I can remember. Do you like the town, Doctor?'

'I like it very much, but obviously it doesn't like me. I'm thinking of throwing in my hand and going back to a hospital.' He was despondent, and there was much in his face to tell Jane of the way he was feeling. She felt a wave of sympathy for him.

'I'm sorry to hear that,' she said slowly. 'If there's anything I can do to help!'

'Thank you, you're very kind!' He smiled fleetingly as he led the way along the hall. 'But I don't think I'm really cut out to be a general practitioner.' He laughed humourlessly. 'Ask some of my patients.'

'What seems to be the trouble?' Jane glanced around the big kitchen which they had entered. It was clean and neat.

'Me, I expect. I'm out of tune with the whole business.' He crossed to a cupboard and brought out a teapot. 'Would you like a cup of tea?'

'Yes, please. I was contemplating dropping in on my uncle, but I expect he's having a doze this afternoon.'

'I don't know how he manages,' Doctor Carson confided as he put on the kettle. 'I'm only half his age, and I feel whacked when each day is done. Then, of course, there are the night calls.'

'Have you no family?' Jane asked. 'Do you live here alone?'

'I'm alone. I don't see a soul, apart from the patients. The woman who does for me comes in when I'm in the surgery, and she's gone by the time I get through in the afternoons.'

'What do you do for meals?' Jane was watching him closely, and she detected the apathy in his tones. Perhaps he was spending too much time alone! It could be most depressing, especially if his every moment was devoted to his patients. There was a lot of truth in the old saying about all work and no play!

'I get by.' He was intent upon his activities, and soon the kettle was boiling. 'I'm not complaining. I can always get out, can't I?'

'But you haven't been here long. Give it a fair chance. You may grow to like it. Look, why don't you come home with me for the evening? I know what it's like to be alone too often. I had some of that while I was away.'

'I couldn't do that,' he said sharply. 'Your parents wouldn't like it if you took home a stranger without warning.'

'Nonsense! You're not a stranger! You're a colleague. There are only three of us in the town! Don't you think we ought to hang together?'

He smiled at her tones, and Jane laughed. Her sympathies were aroused, and she wanted to help him. If no one had held out a friendly hand to him since his arrival, then there was something severely lacking in the town, and she would do what she could to make it up to him. They drank tea together, and he seemed more cheerful as he showed her over the house. He had bought it as it stood, with all of Doctor Wyatt's furniture and collections, and he hadn't bothered to change anything.

'I always liked this house,' Jane told him cheerfully as they went into the front lounge. The strong sunlight was beating against the drawn blinds, and he crossed the room and let the light in. There was an atmosphere of the house being unlived in, despite his presence, and Jane knew he was feeling real loneliness. 'Look, I don't want to be thought interfering,' she said, 'but I wish you would accept my invitation. I'm doing nothing for the rest of the day.' She had a thought, as she spoke, of Steve Denny, and realised that he was calling for her that evening, but she tightened her lips against the knowledge, and knew she could make a quick phone call to put it off. This was for a good cause. A colleague was needing a hand, and she didn't intend to turn her back on him.

'Well, if you think your parents wouldn't mind,' he said slowly.

'They certainly won't.' Jane was reassuring. 'I'm so glad I saw you today. It's dreadful to spend a beautiful day like this on your own. You need a break, don't you?'

'I certainly do.' He nodded slowly, his

blue eyes regarding her lovely face, and he could see the determination that was in her. 'It's very kind of you to take pity on me.'

'Pity!' She shook her head. 'You don't want pity. All you need is company.'

'You're very observant. No doubt you're wondering why I'm in this state of affairs.' He shrugged slightly. 'I lived with my mother until she died recently. That's when I decided to take on a general practice, but it seems I've made a mistake.'

'I wouldn't say that!' Jane was certain she could cheer him up. 'If you're not doing anything in particular now, then why don't you come out with me? I was taking a drive before going home to tea. I had to refresh my mind with the villages we cover, because I'll be doing the rounds as from tomorrow.'

'We'll probably see a lot of each other on the roads,' he retorted. 'I'm always running about out there.'

'I'll wave to you as we pass,' Jane

said, and he laughed, a pleasant sound that made Jane feel happier. His face was showing animation now, and she was pleased.

'I'm glad you've come back to the area,' he said. 'I haven't seen so much friendliness since I got here.'

'Everybody is too busy these days to take the time to wish a stranger well,' she said, knowing that usually she was just as guilty as the next person.

He agreed as they left the house, and Jane watched him as he locked the heavy door. She had been thinking of him ever since that morning, and it seemed too good to be true that she was now in his company. Her memory had not played her false, she thought remotely. He was as handsome as she imagined from their brief encounter the day before, and he was a lot younger-looking when he smiled. She had the feeling he didn't smile too often, and it was probable that he still grieved over the loss of his mother. She wondered about that, and her active mind was thrusting up all sorts of explanations for his failure to get married. She had heard of daughters staying home to take care of a parent, but sons usually married and let their wives do the necessary.

When they were seated in her car he glanced at her. She felt her heart miss a beat as their eyes fixed glances. He smiled, and Jane caught her breath as a wave of emotion struck her. She was feeling very sympathetic towards him. It had struck her yesterday with great force.

'I appreciate this,' he remarked. 'I expect when you were younger you used to take home lame dogs and sick animals, didn't you?'

'As a matter of fact, I did, but I wouldn't class you in the same category.' Jane smiled cheerfully as she drove out of town. There was a small, insistent voice inside her that kept informing her this was a most impor-tant day, but she couldn't for the life of her discover why. They chatted as she drove to the farm, and when they arrived it was to find her parents out.

'It's never wise to bring home guests uninvited,' he said.

'Nonsense. Just make yourself comfortable in here.' Jane opened the door of the lounge and ushered him in. 'I'll have a word with Mrs Gartside and find out what my parents are doing. Mother didn't say anything earlier about going out, but I didn't see Father, and probably he had made arrangements without telling her. He's always doing it. Some men just can't be taught.'

He smiled as she left him, and Jane sought out the housekeeper. Mrs Gartside was a tall, heavily built woman in her late fifties, and a thoroughly efficient housekeeper. She had been with the family for as long as Jane could remember, and they always, got on well together.

'Mrs Gartside, do you know where Mother and Father have done?' Jane enquired, entering the large, modernised kitchen.

'They've gone into town to have tea with Doctor Ashford, Jane. I'm to ask you to go along there.'

'But I have Doctor Carson with me.' Jane pursed her lips. 'I'd better ring them and find out what's doing.'

'What's he like?' Mrs Gartside demanded.

'Doctor Carson?' Jane smiled. 'He's very nice.'

'I've heard tell that he drinks at times. That isn't right for a doctor, is it?'

'Not when he's on duty. But I expect there's a lot of gossip going around about him. It's usually the case when a man is a stranger and not generally liked. Can you tell me why people don't like him, Mrs Gartside?'

'I have no idea. He isn't my doctor, obviously, but I have heard tales that you wouldn't want me to repeat. You never were one for listening to gossip, Jane, and I'm sure you won't start now.'

'That's right.' Jane nodded emphatically. 'I'll ring Uncle John, but I rather think I'll stay here with Doctor Carson. Perhaps you'll get us some tea if we do, will you?'

'Yes, dear.' Mrs Gartside smiled. 'But I'd better warn you that Steve Denny rang up about half an hour ago, saying that he would be out to pick you up at seven.'

'I'll have to ring Steve as well,' Jane said firmly. 'This is getting complicated.'

She went out to the hall, calling Steve first, and his voice was eager as he replied.

'Steve, I'm sorry, but we'll have to postpone tonight's date,' she said, without giving herself time to think. 'You won't mind, will you? We can make it some other evening.'

'No trouble, is there?' he demanded.

'No, but you know how it is. I'm starting work tomorrow. My parents have gone to Uncle John's for tea, and I'm expected to show my face. There are some details I have to go over with Uncle John. We won't have time for them tomorrow.'

'I do mind,' came the stern reply, 'but I also understand, so I'll let you off the hook for once. But don't make a habit of it, Jane. I really do want to take you out.'

'There'll be no trouble next time,' she promised. 'Thank you for being so understanding, Steve. Goodbye.'

'Goodbye,' he replied, and there was regret in his voice.

Jane sighed heavily as she dialled her uncle's number, and a few moments later John Ashford spoke to her.

'John, this is Jane. I've just come home to find that Mother and Father are having tea with you.'

'So what's the problem?' he demanded. 'Come right over.'

'I met Doctor Carson earlier, and invited him here to tea with Mother and Father.'

'Doctor Carson!' There was faint surprise in his voice. 'What are you doing with the opposition, Jane?' He chuckled. 'I haven't met him yet, so you're a pretty fast worker, my girl. Bring him along with you. I'd like to have a chat with him. I ought to have seen him before this, I know, but what with one thing and another I didn't get around to it.'

'I don't know if he'll come. He seems rather quiet. I'll ask him, John, and ring you back. That all right?'

'Anything that you do is all right by me,' came the firm reply.

Jane smiled as she hung up, and she took a deep breath before going into the lounge. Her guest was studying the paintings on the walls, and he turned to comment on them as Jane entered. She paused as she closed the door, taking a good long look at him, and it was as if they were not strangers. There seemed to be a strong compulsion inside Jane, pushing her towards him as she had never moved towards any man before.

'I'm sorry about this afternoon,' she said. 'But this always happens if one doesn't make plans. Mother and Father have gone to my uncle's for tea, and they want me to join them. I rang to tell them I have you with me, and my uncle says to take you along. Do you feel like facing him? We can stay here if you wish, if you won't mind my company alone.'

'That's entirely up to you,' he replied. 'I'm sorry I've messed up your day. Why don't you drop me off at my place on your way to your uncle's?'

'Certainly not. You're stuck with me now. You don't want to go back to your empty house, do you?'

'I'm not keen,' he admitted. 'Let's go to your uncle's then. I would like to meet him. I've got to start making an effort to settle in here, haven't I?'

'You certainly have! And I'll do what I can to help. I'll just ring John again and tell him to expect us. Next time you'll get an invitation to come, and there won't be any complications.'

His smile rewarded her, and Jane went out to the hall to make the call. She did not stop to analyse the feelings inside her, and all she knew was that she felt happy because she was helping him. Having completed her arrangements with John, she went to inform Mrs Gartside of her plans, and then went for Doctor Carson. He seemed quite happy as they drove back to Haylingford.

'By the way,' he observed suddenly as they entered the town. 'My name is Philip. There's no need for us to remain formal, is there?'

'No reason at all. I'm Jane,' she told him, and was rewarded with a smile.

When they reached John's house, Jane felt a momentary panic that was quite unreasonable, but she controlled herself as they entered, and John himself came to greet them. Jane made the introduction, and watched both Philip and her uncle in the first few moments.

'I'm very happy to meet you,' Philip said quietly, shaking hands with John.

'My dear chap, I'm so very sorry that I haven't got around to calling on you before this,' John replied. 'It was too bad of me, I know. But now Jane is on my strength I shall be able to take things a little easier. We must get together and talk about our business here in the town. I do know you're losing patients, because they're coming to me. Is there anything I can help or advise on?'

'Perhaps there is,' Philip said in pleased tones. 'I've put it down to being a stranger and all alone.' He glanced at Jane and she felt her heart turn over with happiness. 'I'll be eternally thankful for the way Jane stepped into the picture.'

'It was the least I could do,' she said demurely. 'There are only the three of us in the area. We ought to be able to pull together, I should think.'

'Well, now isn't the time to go into that,' John announced, 'but I will say here that there is an idea in the back of my mind which may need careful consideration. Let's make a tentative appointment for meeting one evening during the week, shall we? What nights do you keep free, Doctor?'

'I'm on call every night,' Philip replied. 'I don't know what arrangements Doctor Wyatt made, but I never have anything else to do, so I'm always standing by.'

'That's exactly what I'm getting at.' John nodded slowly. 'The sooner we get together the better.'

'What exactly have you in mind, John?' Jane demanded.

'It's something that's happening in a lot of places right now, where doctors are forgetting that generally they are old-fashioned and stick-in-the-mud.' His dark eyes glinted as he stared at Jane. 'Group practice, my dear.'

Jane saw animation come to Philip's face, and she nodded to herself. It sounded like a good idea to her. She moistened her lips as she spoke.

'There's quite a lot to be said for it,' she agreed. 'I haven't had any experience in general practice yet, but I've spoken to quite a lot of young doctors, and they're all agreed that group practice is the coming thing.' She studied Philip's face. 'Tomorrow I shall be going around the villages in our area to see the patients, and I suppose you'll be doing the same thing.'

'That's right.' He nodded. 'Duplication of essential service, isn't it?'

'Well, I'm open to talks on the subject,' John said with a smile. 'I don't know what Jane thinks of it, but she can consider it during the next few days. What do you say to meeting here on Wednesday evening?'

'I'll look forward to it,' Philip said instantly, and Jane nodded eagerly.

'Then it's a firm appointment.' John took Jane's arm. 'Now, let's get off the subject for a bit and join your mother and father, Jane. They'll think I'm a nice one, leaving them alone. Have you met them yet, Philip?'

'I've met Mrs Ashton,' came the steady reply. 'I broke down yesterday near the farm, and walked in to beg use of the telephone.'

'Then come and meet my brother

Charles. You'll find him an interesting chap.'

Jane was strangely lighthearted as they went into the large sitting-room, and the animation in Philip's face told her that she had done the right thing for him. The dejection which had been apparent in him when she saw him earlier was now gone, and there was such a sense of relief for him in her heart that she felt quite unsettled herself. She found herself hoping that Philip Carson would find life interesting, after all, and if there was any way in which she could help him, then she would be ready!

4

By the time Sunday evening drew to a close, Jane felt that she had learned quite a lot about Philip. Her parents seemed to understand that she was filled with a desire to help this handsome doctor, and they made him at ease and extended to him an invitation to visit them at the farm whenever he wished. Jane could see the change which had come to Philip, and she was intensely happy as she insisted upon driving him home. Her parents went back to the farm, and John was ready to go to bed as he saw them to the door.

'Don't be late in the morning, Jane,' he joked. 'A doctor must be punctual in all things.'

'I can't wait to get started,' Jane said with a laugh. 'This is a happy day for me, John. It's been a long time coming, but at last it's here. I feel on top of the world.'

'Perhaps you won't feel so eager when your telephone gets you out of bed at two in the morning, especially in winter, and you drive about five miles to find it's a false alarm, or quite unnecessary,' came the dry retort.

'I'll take all that in my stride,' Jane said. 'How do you feel about it, Philip?'

'I'm a dedicated man,' he replied, nodding. 'I don't mind in the least.'

'So there are two dedicated doctors in town,' John mused lightly. 'I suppose I'd better say that I'm dedicated, too.'

'There's no need for you to say anything,' Jane retorted. 'You've proved yourself over the years. Philip and I have to make ourselves known and build reputations.'

'And I haven't made a very good start,' Philip said. 'But that will change now, I assure you.'

'That's good news.' John was suddenly serious. 'Don't hesitate to call me if there's any way I can help, Philip. I mean that, so bear it in mind, won't you?'

'I shall, and thank you very much.' Sincerity rang in his tones.

'Now, good night.' John stepped off the threshold and started closing the door. 'Don't forget about Wednesday evening.'

'I won't let him forget,' Jane said firmly.

She was happy as they walked out to her car, and they drove to Philip's house. When she drew up at the kerb outside his gate he turned to her, and she could see a shining happiness in his face.

'I don't know how to thank you,' he said slowly. 'I was down in the dumps when we met this afternoon. For two pins I would have thrown up the practice and gone away with my tail between my legs.'

'And now?' she queried.

'I feel like a new man.' He smiled gently. 'I have to live somewhere, and running away from Haylingford would only make matters worse.'

'Why running away?' she asked. 'I'm sure you're a very good doctor.'

'You're sure of quite a lot of things,' he responded. 'I don't know quite what to make of you, Jane. You're an angel, among other things, and meeting you has put a ray of light into my life.'

'Glad I was able to help,' she said lightly. 'I just put myself in your place, and I wouldn't have wanted to face prospects like those. I'm glad you're feeling more settled now. Loneliness is a dreadful predicament.'

'My fault, of course,' he replied slowly. 'I wasn't prepared to give myself a chance, until you came along.'

'And what do you think of John's suggestion for a group practice?' She found herself hanging on breathlessly for his answer.

'It's a jolly good idea. Do you think anything will come of it?'

'I hope so. It will mean we can give a better service to the public. They won't have to sit around in the waiting-rooms so long. And for ourselves it means a considerable saving. We'll get more time off. That old business of a doctor being on call twenty-four hours a day, seven days a week, deserves to die the death. We're only human beings, and if we're to give of our best then we have to take care of ourselves. I'm all for it, Philip.'

'Then we'll see what comes of it,' he retorted, nodding. 'For myself, I can only gain from the association. Your uncle will most probably find it difficult giving up the habits and routine of a lifetime.'

'And I don't start until tomorrow,' Jane said, nodding. 'I'm very much an untried specimen in this field.'

'I don't doubt that you'll prove an invaluable practitioner,' he told her with a smile. 'You certainly have all the qualities. I'm never going to forget you, Jane.' He drew a sharp breath and sighed heavily. 'Now I'd better go in. You'll probably find it a heavy day tomorrow. But let me thank you for what you've done. I feel a different man already. I'm in your debt, so don't forget to let me know if there's anything I can ever do for you.'

'I'll bear that in mind.' Jane was happy as she smiled. 'I like doing things for people, so don't worry that you owe me a favour.'

'Good night, and I'll see you on Wednesday evening at your uncle's house.'

'I'll be there.' Jane felt a pang of disappointment that she was not going to see him before then, but she quickly smothered it. 'Good night, Philip.'

He got out of the car and waved a hand to her as he closed his gate. Jane waved cheerily, and drove away with something like a song in her heart. She was satisfied with the knowledge that it had been a day well spent. Driving home, she felt tired but happy, and there was every indication that this new phase of her life would unfold favourably.

At home, her mother was waiting up for her, and Jane sat down with a cup of coffee. Her mother was watching her closely, and when Jane caught her eye she smiled.

'I like Doctor Carson, Jane. He's a very nice young man. I'm so glad John is going to talk about a group practice. I think it is the best thing that could happen. You did the right thing in bringing them together.'

'At the moment I'm glad I did, Mother,' Jane replied. 'All I hope is that I won't live to regret it. There's a big danger in trying to shape other people's lives, isn't there?'

'Sometimes it pays to lend a helping hand,' Mrs Ashford said with a smile. 'The only danger in that sort of thing is most people tend to overdo it. But if you leave well alone now, I don't think you need have cause for concern.'

Jane was satisfied, and shortly went to bed. She lay for some time thinking about the events of the day and considering what might turn up on the morrow, but eventually she slept, to awake at seven next morning to a sunny day.

At breakfast she sat with her mother, always an early riser. Her father had gone out to do a round of the farm, and Jane felt butterflies inside as she prepared to face the day's work. But she was confident, and brimming with happiness. She was impatient to start, and long before it was really necessary she was taking her medical bag out to the car. As she kissed her mother goodbye, Mrs Ashford hugged her warmly.

'Good luck, Jane. I hope it will go right for you.'

'Thank you, Mother. This is the happiest day of my life. I'll give you a ring during the morning. I don't know what time I'll get home to lunch. John did say I was to take the surgery this morning, but if I come home to lunch I might be able to save him a couple of calls in this area.'

'Don't worry about anything. Lunch will be here when you return.'

Jane nodded and got into her car. She drove merrily to town, and parked in the small yard behind the surgeries. She sighed deeply to dispel her nervousness as she carried her bag into the building, and she was in time to hear Milly Andrews telling a patient that Doctor Jane Ashford was taking surgery this morning.

'Up the stairs and in the waiting-room on the left,' the receptionist said cheerfully, and looked up to see Jane standing there. 'Good morning, Doctor Ashford. You're early.'

'Good morning, Milly.' Jane smiled as the patient turned to look curiously at her. It was a man with a very swollen left eye, and Jane thought he had been in a fight. But he went up the stairs to the waiting-room as she entered the receptionist's office. 'Is my uncle around yet?' she queried.

'He rang a few moments ago, and said he'd be in shortly. I've put the panel records on your desk of the people you have to see this morning.'

'Then I'll go up and make a start.' Jane left the office and walked up the stairs. She glanced into the waiting-room and called a cheery good morning to the half-dozen patients seated there. In her surgery she settled down, and then rang for the first patient.

A woman came into the room, and Jane bade her sit down, aware that this was her very first patient in the practice. She smiled as the woman studied her, and looked at the card Milly had supplied.

'What's the trouble?' she asked. 'It's Mrs Baines, isn't it?'

'I've got this cough, Doctor. It isn't much. Seems rather a nervous cough, and it's irritating. My husband insisted that I came in.'

'Have you had a cold?' Jane questioned, reading the details of previous treatment from the card. 'I see you've had this cough for some time. Hasn't the medicine you were given done any good?'

'It eased it until the medicine was

gone.' Mrs Baines was a small, nervous woman. 'My husband thinks it's something more serious. I haven't had a cold since last winter.'

'And was the cough worse then?'

'Not really.'

'I see.' Jane got to her feet and walked around the desk. 'Let me have a look at your throat, Mrs Baines.'

She examined the throat, and then felt gently with probing fingers. Mrs Baines watched her with anxious eyes.

'There's a lump here,' Jane said. 'Does it hurt?'

'Only when you press it. I've had that for a long time. It's not cancer, is it?'

Jane went back to the desk and sat down. She smiled reassuringly. 'I think we'll send you to see a specialist,' she decided. 'There's nothing to worry about, Mrs Baines. I think you have a goitre. It isn't serious, but it's causing that cough you complain of.' She busied herself writing a letter, and Mrs Baines watched her in shocked silence. When Jane sealed the letter in an envelope, the woman took it reluctantly.

'Will I have to go into hospital, Doctor?' she demanded. 'It couldn't be cancer, could it? What shall I do about my family? I'll have no one to look after them.'

'Don't worry, Mrs Baines. It isn't serious. Go along to the hospital and give them this letter, and you'll see a specialist. I assure you there's nothing to really worry about.'

'All right, Doctor, and I do hope you're right. But anything will be better than having this cough, and when I lie down it's just as if a weight is pressing down on my throat. I have such a job to breathe properly.'

Jane smiled consolingly, and ushered the woman out. She made an entry on the card before ringing for the next patient. Her butterflies were gone now, and her hands were quite steady. The next patient was a man, and he paused in the doorway to stare at her.

'Come in and sit down, Mr Weston.' Jane glanced at the card before her.

'I wanted to see Doctor Ashford,' he said firmly.

'I am Doctor Ashford.' Jane smiled.

'I want to see your uncle, Doctor,' he retorted. 'When will he be here?'

'This evening, but I assure you I'm quite capable. Won't you tell me what's troubling you?'

'It's my chest, but I'm not having you pulling me about. All I need is some medicine. You'll have details on that card about the stuff I usually get.' He didn't come towards the desk, but remained by the door, staring at her as if he had never seen a woman doctor before.

Jane looked at the card, then nodded. 'Are you off work, Mr Weston.'

'No. I'm not one of those lay-abouts, although I could be if I wanted to. I've seen people a lot better off than me swinging the lead.' He paused and coughed hackingly.

'What sort of work do you do?' Jane asked.

'I'm a road sweeper. Plenty of fresh

air.' He was tall and powerfully built, in his fifties. 'Nothing will ever cure me, and I make the best of it. Your uncle usually writes out a prescription so I can pick it up without bothering to come in here and wait to see someone.'

'I see. Well, as this is my first day here, Mr Weston, I want to see all the patients as they come in. But I'll give you a prescription. Do you find the medicine helps you at all?'

'Oh, yes. It's all right. Perhaps I ought to get it by the gallon. It would save all this running in and out every other week.'

'But we have to see you from time to time,' Jane pointed out, scribbling the prescription.

He came forward to take it quickly, and then he was gone, and she sighed as she looked at the next card. When she rang for another patient, Milly followed the man with the swollen eye into the room, and the girl put down four more panel records.

'Doctor Ashford has just come in,'

she reported. 'He wants to know how you're getting on.'

'Tell him it's all right,' Jane replied, and the receptionist went out. Jane looked at the man seated on the chair. His left eye was inflamed, but it wasn't bruised as she had at first thought.

'I don't have to tell you what my trouble is, do I, Doctor?' he demanded. 'It's been like this for a couple of days. It just came up. It doesn't even hurt.'

Jane went around the desk to examine the eye. 'Mr Garner, isn't it?' she demanded, and he nodded. 'Well, this is cystic inflammation. You have a cyst in that upper eyelid.'

'It doesn't hurt!' he said quickly. 'What can you do for it?'

'I'll give you some ointment.' Jane sat down again and drew the prescription pad before her. 'I want this ointment to go under the lid as well as on the outside,' she said.

'Will it clear up by itself?' he asked, taking the form.

'I'm hoping it will, but it may get bigger, and if it does you'll have to come and see me again, Mr Garner.'

'Then what will happen?' he demanded.

'It can easily be removed. It's nothing serious.'

'Thank you, Doctor.' He nodded. 'I hope it won't come to that.'

Jane wrote down the particulars of treatment as he departed, and then rang for the next patient. She began to get into the routine, and when she reached the last card on the desk, and dealt with the patient, she glanced at her watch and was surprised to see the time was almost eleven. She sat back in her seat for a moment and relaxed. Then she lifted the receiver of the telephone and spoke to Molly, who assured her there were no more patients.

'I'll bring the cards down for you, Milly,' she said, and hung up.

Going down to the receptionist's office, she arrived in time to take the telephone receiver from Milly.

'It's Doctor Ashford,' the girl whispered.

'Hello, John,' Jane said.

'How are you doing, Jane?' came the reply.

'I've just finished. Is there anything I can help you with? I shall be going home to lunch, and I can make any calls around Winchley, to save you some mileage.'

'Thank you very much for the offer, but having started the round at the time I usually sit down in the surgery, I'm almost done. Normally I would be just starting out on the round. If this morning is anything to work on, I wish I had taken a partner years ago.'

'I'm glad you think I'm an asset,' Jane told him with a laugh.

'I passed Doctor Carson this morning, Jane,' her uncle went on. 'We didn't have a chance to talk about yesterday. But we'll get together before we see him on Wednesday evening. I'm afraid I rather sprang that group practice business on you without prior warning.

But how did it strike you?'

'I like the idea,' she said promptly.

'Because you like Doctor Carson?' he demanded.

'No. I wouldn't let personal feelings influence me in any way, John.'

'I know that, Jane. I'm just ribbing you. But he's a nice young man. I had imagined him to be a lot different, from the various stories I've heard. But one can't always go by appearances or rumours. I'm glad you brought him around yesterday.'

'Let's hope it will all work out right,' Jane said.

'I'm sure it will. But we'll talk later. I'll get on with what I have to do, and I'll drop in at the farm before coming back to town.'

'Shall I see you there?' Jane demanded. 'I want to ask you about evening surgery, and who will be standing by for emergency calls.'

'I'll wait until you get home,' he said. 'But offhand I'd say it will be better for the one who takes morning surgery to be on call during the day and the evening. The other will handle the rounds and take evening surgery. Does that sound feasible to you?'

'Certainly. And we'll change duties daily, shall we?'

'That's the idea. Then instead of getting one evening off a week, we shall have every other evening off.'

'Sounds all right,' Jane said brightly. 'See you later, John.'

The line went dead, and Jane hung up. Milly smiled at her.

'I'm so glad everything is going all right,' the girl said. 'I know Doctor Ashford has been waiting such a long time for you to come here. I'm sure he won't be disappointed with the arrangements.'

'Well, I've had an easy morning,' Jane said. 'Was that the usual number of patients I had this morning?'

'Yes. There's never so very many during the summer. But the waiting-room will be crowded in winter, I expect.'

'That's still quite some way off,' Jane retorted. 'I ought to have settled down by then. I'll go and tidy up the surgery, and then I'll push off. I can see that Uncle John was hard pressed working the practice alone. No wonder a lot of practices are forming into groups.'

'Do you think it could ever happen here?' Milly demanded. 'I have seen Doctor Carson, and he's very attractive.'

'I have met him.' Jane smiled. 'But some of his patients don't like him.'

'It isn't him personally, from what I hear. A lot of people are missing old Doctor Wyatt.'

Jane nodded. That was her explanation for the problem that faced Philip. She pictured him, and knew impatience when she recalled that she wouldn't be seeing him before Wednesday evening.

'I shall be on call for the rest of the day and through the night,' she told Milly. 'What arrangements do you make about that?'

'All calls are sent through to the

doctor's house when the surgery is closed,' Milly said. 'We'll have to inform the exchange that you're taking over, and the patients will get your number when they ask. I'll have the information put up in the waiting-rooms, and in a short time everyone will know the form.'

'Good. I wouldn't want Uncle John to get called out in the middle of the night when I ought to go.'

'There won't be any trouble,' Milly said confidently. 'I'm here all day, and any calls that come in after the doctor has started his round will be classed as emergency. So today you'll be attending. If you do go off anywhere, perhaps you'll let me know your whereabouts so I can reach you.'

'Of course. I shall have to get into the habit of doing that, just in case.' Jane nodded. 'I'm going home now. I ought to be there in about fifteen minutes. But if I don't get any calls, I won't have anything to do for the rest of the day. What about clinics, Milly? And what else is there to do?'

'Clinics are Tuesdays and Thursdays, and dental duties come on Wednesdays and Fridays.'

'I must talk to my uncle about that side of it,' Jane said, nodding. 'All right, Milly. I'll pack up and go. You know where to find me.'

'Yes, Doctor.' The girl nodded.

Jane went up to her surgery and tidied the place. She stood at the window for some moments gazing along the street, and there was firm knowledge inside her that this work was going to agree with her. But while she stood idle, her mind turned to Philip Carson, and a picture of his face flashed before her. She smiled tenderly. It was nice to know that he was there in the background. She was completely taken up with the practice at the moment, but a part of her mind had set itself aside to deal with Philip. She was looking forward to Wednesday night! That much was very clear to her, and if she had nothing to do this evening then perhaps she could ring him to learn how he had been making out!

She was slightly surprised at the way he had seemed to flit into her life without any period of seeming a stranger. She felt that she had known him for years, and it came to her that she understood him better than she understood Steve Denny or Roger Keeble, although she had practically grown up with the both of them. But her surprise was pleasant, and she had the feeling that something very important was on the horizon, just waiting to come upon her.

5

The next two days passed well, and Jane began to settle into the practice. She attended at the surgery and did the country rounds. Her days were busy and eventful, and she was thoroughly pleased with the situation. On Wednesday evening she went to John's house with a great feeling of anticipation gripping her. She had not seen Philip since Sunday, and she wanted to meet him again. She had been vaguely surprised that he hadn't contacted her, but there was plenty of time, she told herself as she drove to town. On the other hand, she had put off Steve Denny again, and refused an offer of a night out with Roger Keeble.

Philip hadn't arrived when she entered John's house, and she chatted with John about the day's work as they waited for Philip to arrive. The time went by, and then the telephone rang. John went in answer, and returned some moments later shaking his head ruefully.

'That was Philip calling,' he said. 'He's gone out on a case, and it's complicated. He's waiting for the ambulance to arrive.'

'Will he be coming later?' Jane demanded, and John nodded.

'He said he would, if we didn't mind waiting. I'm not going anywhere myself, and I have the feeling that you would wait a long time for Philip Carson, Jane.'

'Don't start jumping to conclusions, John,' Jane warned with a smile.

'I wouldn't dream of it,' he retorted, but his brown eyes were twinkling. 'Anyway, we can discuss this group practice business, can't we? I've been putting in a lot of thought, as it is, and I want to try some of the ideas out on you.'

'Go ahead, but remember that I'm new to this business.'

'You're working like an old hand,' he retorted. 'I must give praise where it is due.'

'Thank you. I appreciate those few kind words. But what this group practice means is that Philip would come into partnership with us and we would handle all the patients between us. Isn't that so?'

'Broadly speaking. We would keep our own patients as far as possible, but there would be three of us in the same block, covering for one another as far as possible. Holidays wouldn't be such a worrying business, and all duties would always be covered. One of us would do the rounds, and the other two would handle the surgeries and emergencies. There would always be two on duty out of the three.'

'It sounds as if it might work very well.' Jane's eyes gleamed as she considered seeing Philip every day of her life.

'We wouldn't have patients coming in and sitting for an hour or so in the waiting-room,' John went on. 'We would work an appointments system. Philip has a receptionist, and she would come to work in our block. There's more than enough room in the building for another surgery. We would have our own separate surgeries, of course.'

'I like the sound of it,' Jane said. 'Why haven't you suggested something like this before?'

'I did, to Doctor Wyatt, but he was an old man well set in his old-fashioned ways. He didn't want to know. Now there's a younger man in his place it can be made to work. It will be easier for all concerned.'

'Well, so far I like everything you've said,' Jane told him. 'I don't see any obstacles. Philip was saying on Sunday evening, after we left here, that he liked the sound of it.'

'Then we'll put it to him in detail and find out what his reactions are.' John nodded eagerly. 'It will take a weight off my mind, I can tell you. I'm beginning to reach the age where I need to take it a bit easy. You're young enough to pull your weight, and Philip seems a decent sort. Perhaps I'm going to be lucky, after all.'

They chatted about the project until the doorbell rang, and John went in answer, to return with Philip at his heels. Jane smiled a warm greeting, and Philip came to say hello.

'I am sorry for being so late,' he apologised.

'Think nothing of it,' John said firmly. 'I've been a doctor for more years than I care to remember, and I can hardly remember the time when I was able to be on time for an appointment. Or if I got there punctually, then you can take it that I was usually called out before time.'

'How have you been getting along since Sunday?' Jane asked, and was rewarded with a smile.

'Very well,' Philip replied. 'I've cheered up no end, and the patients are beginning to notice it. But you have some business to talk over with me.'

'It's about this group practice,' John said. 'Jane and I have talked it over and she's struck on the idea.' He began to outline the situation, and Jane watched Philip's face closely, intent upon gaining his reactions. From time to time he glanced at her, obviously aware of her presence, and she felt her pulses beat faster as she studied him. Her mind had retained exactly the details of his features, and she could feel an attraction forming inside her. But she forced herself to concentrate upon what John was saying, and he ended as she glanced at him. 'That's the situation as I see it,' he said. 'Think it over, Philip, and then let us know what you decide. As far as I can see, there are plenty of advantages and very few disadvantages.'

'I don't need to think it over,' Philip said instantly. 'Or I ought to say that I have been thinking it over, and I've come to the conclusion that group practices are the *in* thing, as the saying goes. If you're prepared to take me in with you, then I'm quite happy about it.

Go right ahead with the details and we'll get the thing started as soon as possible.'

'There's enough room in our surgery block for you,' John said. 'You could be on the top floor with Jane. I'm getting too old to climb stairs at my age. What do you say? Shall we start operations?'

'Yes,' Philip said without hesitation. 'Are you happy about it, Jane?'

'Very happy,' she replied.

'There is one thing,' Philip said. 'I have a receptionist at my surgery. What happens to her?'

'We shall need two receptionists at least,' John said. 'She'll merely switch places of work. But you must come around to our place and look it over, tell me what you think of it.'

'I've got nothing on for the rest of the evening,' Jane said almost without thinking. 'If you care to strike while the iron is hot, then I'll show you around now.'

'I like someone who doesn't waste time,' Philip said, smiling. 'All right, so let's go and look.'

'Come back later, if you wish, and I'll have some coffee ready,' John offered.

'Thanks, I could do with some company,' Philip said, and Jane felt her pulses leap as his blue eyes caught her glance.

'Good. We'll have to get together a lot more often,' John said. He glanced at Jane with a glint in his dark eyes. 'But I'm sure Jane would be more suitable company for you. She doesn't have a boyfriend, to my certain knowledge, and it's about time she started living a social life. It's all very well being dedicated to your profession, but all work and no play, as the saying goes.'

'Well, perhaps we can do something about that.' Philip smiled as he escorted Jane towards the door. 'What do you say?' he asked her.

'Yes.' She found difficulty in getting the word out, but she was very pleased as they went out to his car.

Philip drove to the surgeries, and Jane fumbled for her keys. They entered and she showed him around the ground floor. There was more than enough room for another receptionist in the office, and Philip commented upon the fact. Then Jane showed him her uncle's suite, and they stood for a moment looking around the place where John Ashford had spent the greater part of his working life.

'Let's go upstairs now,' Jane said. 'My surgery and waiting-room are up there, and yours will be across the corridor from mine. The whole place has recently been redecorated, so there's none of that inconvenience to suffer.'

'I've been working from the house,' Philip said. 'It was the custom in the old days, but I don't really approve of it. This is something totally different, and I'm greatly in favour of it.'

They went up to the top floor and Jane showed him around. The surgery which would be his was bare but clean, and he nodded as he looked around. There was a smaller room beyond, which could be made into an examination-room, and Jane knew he was pleased as they went to look at her surgery.

'Very nice indeed,' he commented. 'We'll have to talk firm details now. How soon do you think we can get started on this idea?'

'As soon as you can move in, I should think,' Jane said eagerly, and saw him smile.

'You're still doing your good neighbour act, Jane,' he said.

'I feel satisfied when I am,' she admitted. 'I like doing a good turn, don't you?'

'I haven't had the chance lately to do anything for anyone.' He smiled thinly. 'But there are prospects.'

A sudden footstep on the stairs outside made Jane start, and she looked around at the door as someone came along the corridor. Philip went to the door and opened it, and Jane peered past him to see Roger Keeble standing outside.

'Hello,' he said, grinning. 'I saw the

lights from the road and guessed it might be you here, Jane.' He looked curiously at Philip, who stepped back out of the doorway.

'Hello, Roger. Not in need of my professional services, are you?' Jane smiled as she went forward. She introduced them to each other, and saw that Philip had become watchful. They shook hands, and Roger nodded slowly.

'So this is why you're always so busy when I ring you,' he commented. 'Do you work night and day every day, Jane?'

'I'm not on duty now,' she replied. 'I'm just showing Doctor Carson around.'

'If everyone was like me, then people like you two would be out of work,' Roger said. 'By the way, Jane, have you been out with Steve yet since you've been back?'

'No. I haven't had the time.' She frowned, aware that Philip was watching her. 'Why?'

'He's moping around wishing that you were a factory girl who had every evening free,' came the grinning reply. 'What have you done to him?'

'I don't know what you mean.' Jane knew she sounded a little bit prim, but she couldn't help it. She knew Roger well enough to realise that he would do anything to create different impressions upon people in order to serve his own ends. Steve had told her that Roger said he was taking her out, no doubt with the intention of steering Steve away from her. Roger was the kind of man who believed in the old saying that all was fair in love and war.

'You never would admit that you've always had half the fellows in this area pining for you,' Roger continued impishly. He was watching Philip, but there was nothing showing in Philip's face to reveal his thoughts.

'It's the first I've heard of it,' Jane replied, laughing. 'What are you trying to do, Roger, ruin my reputation?'

'A doctor's reputation is the most important thing in the world,' Philip said thinly.

'I agree with you.' Jane moved towards the door. 'We were just leaving, Roger.'

'Going on to some slick night club?' Roger demanded.

'Around here?' Philip countered.

'No, we're going back to my uncle's to talk business,' Jane said quickly.

'Then I won't delay you. But I'll tell Steve I've seen you.' Roger turned away. 'Good night,' he called over his shoulder, and Jane echoed the word with thankfulness.

They remained on the top floor until Roger had left, and the silence that surrounded them was heavy with unspoken feeling. Then Jane led the way down, and they locked up and went out to Philip's car. As they drove back to John's home, Jane felt she ought to remark upon Roger.

'You shouldn't place any weight upon what he says,' she said slowly. 'The other evening he told Steve Denny he had a date with me, to stop Steve asking me out. That's the kind of man Roger is.'

Philip made no comment, and they went into John's to find coffee waiting for them. Philip seemed quiet as they talked out the final details, but Jane was hopeful as they agreed to try the group practice idea, and John promised to put the plan into execution immediately. They decided upon a date a month hence for the change to be made, and Jane mentally crossed her fingers as she hoped that nothing would prevent the whole affair becoming reality.

When Philip got up to leave, Jane moved also. John saw them to the door, and Jane knew he was happy with their arrangements. She could not tell from Philip's face what he was really thinking, but they stood by her car and chatted about the prospects. Finally, he glanced at his watch.

'It's time to go,' he said. 'But before you leave me, is there any chance we can get together one evening?'

'I don't see why not!' Jane felt a pang strike through her, and she breathed a little faster. 'I expect we'll both be off duty at the same time in the next day or two.'

'I'm free on Friday,' he said quickly. 'Can you make it then?'

'I expect so.' Jane did some mental calculations. 'Yes. I shall be free.'

'Then perhaps we can go for a drive and have dinner somewhere. I'm a stranger around here, but you'll probably know the best spots.'

'I'm not sure of that,' Jane said with a laugh. 'I was never one for a lot of pleasure. You should discount anything that Roger Keeble said.'

'I already have.' Philip nodded. 'Shall I call for you at the farm?'

'I can drive in, if you wish,' she offered.

'No. I think I'd better do it in style. I'll call for you about seven.'

'I'll be ready,' Jane promised.

He smiled and took his leave, and Jane got into her car, to watch him drive away. She sighed as she pulled away from the kerb, and her thoughts were not on her driving as she left town. There was a growing optimism inside her that knew no bounds. Everything was working out very satisfactorily. But she pulled herself up abruptly. What was happening in the dim recesses of her mind? Why was she feeling so hopeful? What did she want from life now that she was settling down in her uncle's practice? Wasn't life offering her enough as it was?

The thoughts were powerful, emotional, and Jane felt that she knew the answers to the pounding questions. She was attracted to Philip. That much was apparent. From the very first moment she had been attracted, like a piece of metal placed too close to a magnet. But now several days had passed and she was begging subconsciously for progress. Friday evening would be a step in the right direction, and it couldn't come quick enough for her. She laughed inwardly as she considered the future. Everything in the garden was lovely!

When she arrived home there was a

large black car parked in the driveway, and she frowned as she recognised it as Steve Denny's. Jane went into the house, to find Steve in the lounge with her father. Steve got to his feet when he saw her, and Jane smiled pleasantly.

'Hello, Steve! Were you looking for me?'

'Yes.' He nodded. 'The days are passing, and I haven't seen anything of you. I was afraid that you'd forget all about me.'

'I told you she's been very busy, Steve,' her father said. 'But excuse me, and I'll find out what your mother is doing, Jane. She's been in the kitchen with Mrs Gartside almost all evening. I don't know if we're going to suffer a whole spate of new recipes, or what is happening, but I have the feeling something is in the wind. Perhaps I'll see you before you leave, Steve. But if I don't, then remember to tell your father about that new cowshed I want put up, will you?'

'Yes, Mr Ashford, you can rely upon

it. I've got the measurements and details, and I'll have some plans ready for you in a couple of weeks.'

'I'm in no real hurry, but I shall need it in use before the winter sets in.' Charles Ashford patted Jane's shoulder and left the room.

'I'm sorry if I seem to be neglecting my old friends, Steve,' Jane said slowly, moving to the sofa. She sat down and he came to her side, taking hold of her hands as he leaned back at her side.

'I know it must be awkward for you, trying to find some spare time for the likes of me,' he retorted. 'But I was speaking to Roger in the Bull's Head about an hour ago, and he said you were out for the evening with that Doctor Carson.'

'You know Roger,' she replied slowly. 'He always did try to cause trouble among the men interested in me. I was with Doctor Carson, but it was strictly business.'

'I believe you.' Steve looked into her

eyes. 'Jane, I have given you some indication of my feelings towards you. I hope I'm not going to be pushed off by pressures arising from meeting new faces.'

'Steve, I warn you that I have no interests outside my work. My plate is rather full at the moment, and nothing else can come into consideration, so please don't start building a future around us. You'll be bound to meet with disappointment.'

'I'm not an impatient man, Jane.' He drew a sharp breath, and the sound of it seemed to fill the room. His dark eyes were large and appealing. 'All I ask is that you don't forget me.'

'I'm not likely to do that.' She smiled, trying to abate the tension that gripped her. 'But I want to impress upon you at the outset that I have no time for romance or anything approaching it, Steve. You know what I mean, don't you?'

'I'm afraid I do, and it isn't very encouraging.' He shook his head slowly.

'Why haven't you bothered with boyfriends, Jane? Do you hate men?'

'No.' She smiled as she thought of Philip. 'I suppose the right one has never come along. I've never been able to flirt like other girls do. I have to like a man a great deal before I can go around with him.'

'You were Roger's girl a long time ago.'

'But that was kid's stuff,' she retorted with a smile. 'Calf love and that sort of thing. I told Roger a long time ago that he and I were poles apart in every way. You must bear that in mind when he tells you things.'

'I don't believe the half of what he says. I never did. But this evening he seemed to think there were stars in your eyes when you were with that new doctor.'

'I never knew Roger when he wasn't exaggerating.' Jane shook her head slowly. 'I think it's psychological with Roger.'

'Then when am I going to see you

again? Can't you find one evening for me?' He stared at her, and his lips tightened when Jane shook her head slowly. 'Your father tells me you're off duty on Friday evening. Can't we get together then?'

'I'm sorry, but I have an engagement on Friday evening.'

'With that doctor!' He sighed heavily, and got to his feet and began to pace the floor. 'Jane, I've been waiting months for you to come home. Now you're here! I thought it would be easy for me to see you. What have I got to do? Should I go sick or something?'

'I'm sorry, Steve, but that's the way it is,' she said, standing up and facing him. 'I don't want to hurt you, but I have no desire to become involved with any man. I hope you'll understand. It's nothing personal, I assure you.'

'All right.' He nodded as he came to stand in front of her. 'I suppose I am trying to rush things. You haven't been back a week yet. But faint heart never won fair lady, and I'm afraid you'll find someone else in the meantime. Promise me you'll keep an open mind, Jane.'

'Steve, I can't promise anything,' she replied, shaking her head. 'It would be unfair for the both of us. Please try to understand. I have so much on my mind at the moment. This is all new work to me, and I have to settle in. There are some more changes coming that will have to be taken into account. I'm sorry if I sound so unapproachable, but that's the situation.'

'All right.' He nodded. 'See me out to my car, will you? I'd better go. But I'll see you again, Jane. Don't neglect me, will you?'

She crossed the room with him and they left the house. The sky was gloomy now, but still clear, and Jane could see the first star glimmering remotely far above. A gentle breeze touched her cheeks. She could smell the flowers in the garden, and peacefulness lay all around in the perfect dusk.

'Jane.' Steve's arms came out of the darkness and wrapped around her. She took a deep breath and tried to push him off, but he held her firmly, with great strength. The next moment he was kissing her, and Jane could smell stale tobacco smoke on him and was revolted. She twisted sharply to get away from him, unable to match his strength, and he hurt her arms and neck with his unyielding strength. But she managed to lower her face, and he rained kisses upon her forehead and hair. 'Jane, I love you!' His words were harsh and intent. 'I can't go on much longer without you. I've loved you for years, but always hid it. You were always so unapproachable, and I've been eating out my heart over you.'

'Let me go, Steve!' she panted. 'Please let me go!'

He did so reluctantly, his arms falling to his sides, and he remained motionless, staring at her, now devoid of all emotion, filled with the bitter emptiness of defeat. Jane felt sorry for him, but his action had aroused her and she was trembling uncontrollably.

'Good night, Steve!' she said, and turned towards the house.

'Wait!' He reached out and grasped her wrist. 'Let me talk to you, Jane, if only to apologise. Don't send me away like this.'

'It's no use, Steve,' she said firmly. 'There can never be anything for us together in the future. It would be better if you accepted that right from the start. I don't want to see you get hurt, but that is what will happen if you don't try to forget me.'

'There must be someone else, for you to talk so firmly about it,' he retorted. 'Is it that new doctor, Jane? Has he attracted you?'

'I don't wish to talk about it.' She tried to pull away from him, but his grip upon her arm was too strong. 'I'm truly sorry you should feel this way about me, Steve, I really am. It can only bring anguish to you.'

He let go of her, but did not move away. Jane was saddened by the knowledge that this would end their friendship. From childhood they had been friends, but this would end all that, and it would mean that a piece of her died in the process.

'Good night, Steve,' she said in quivering tones. 'I must go in now.'

'Good night,' he replied thickly, and turned away to get into his car. The next instant he was speeding away down the lane, and Jane froze as she heard his brakes squeal when he reached the turning. His rear lights brightened, then dimmed, and he was gone.

As silence returned, Jane walked slowly to the house and entered. She closed the door and tried to shut outside the nagging doubts that suddenly assailed her. Why had she been so definite in her refusal to become involved with Steve? She had always liked him. He was a prize for any girl. What was there in her that had rejected him so completely? She had been sickened by their contact. Had his query about her being a man-hater any truth in it? She was suddenly filled with strange doubts.

Was there something wrong with her? She felt normal, and had strong feelings for Philip. But she had never accustomed herself to going around with boys when she had been younger. She had never been happy suffering their kisses. Of course, she had been all right with Roger Keeble, but she had used his running around with other girls as an excuse to break with him. Since Roger there had been no one of any importance.

Jane went to bed in thoughtful mood, trying to analyse herself, but where she might have been able to help a patient in the same straits she could not make any headway with herself. All she succeeded in doing was to fill herself with nagging doubt and indecision . . .

6

By Friday evening Jane was filled with a strange eagerness to see Philip again. She had pushed into the background all the troublesome thoughts of herself, and the doubts were buried under a coating of anticipation. After a busy day she prepared to go out for the evening, and when she was ready she told her mother where she was going and with whom.

'I think you're doing the right thing by making a friend of Philip Carson,' Mrs Ashford commented. 'I like him, Jane, and I can usually tell about people.'

'He seems to be so lonely,' Jane said slowly, wondering why she had to justify herself. 'From what I've gathered in conversation, he used to live alone with his mother, until she died. He was in a bad way last Sunday when I saw him, but I managed to cheer him up.'

'I should think you're capable of cheering up anyone with no trouble at all,' her mother replied, staring intently at Jane's flushed face and pleasure-filled eyes. 'I'm really proud of you, Jane. You've turned out a real credit to us in every way.'

'Did you ever have any doubts, Mother?' There was a half-smile on Jane's lips and a quizzical light in her eyes.

'Certainly not! But you've done even better than I expected. I think John had more foresight than any of us, to see that you could become a doctor. He talked of nothing else for years, but I never expected you to fall in with his wishes. Are you really happy with yourself, Jane?'

'More happy than I could ever be doing something different,' Jane retorted. 'All's right with my world, Mother.'

'Good. I'm very glad to hear it.' Mrs Ashford turned to the high window and peered out across the gardens at the driveway. 'I hear a car coming,' she informed. 'I expect it will be your date.'

Jane crossed to her mother's side, filled with many emotions. She saw Philip's car coming towards the house, and a warm feeling surged through her. He had been very lonely last week, she knew, and she so wanted to help him. He was doing a very responsible job, and it seemed dreadful to her that no one was bothered about him. But she cared. The thought was strong inside her, and Jane kissed her mother's cheek and prepared to depart.

'Have a nice time, dear,' Mrs Ashford said.

'Thanks, Mother, I will,' Jane replied.

She was conscious of brimming happiness as she left the house, and Philip got out of the car to greet her. He was smiling, and looked very much happier than he had been the previous Sunday.

'Hello, Jane,' he said almost shyly. 'Thought I wasn't coming? I was about to leave, when I found I had a flat tyre. I changed the wheel and dropped into the garage to get it checked. Can't take any chances with a thing like that. I'll pick up the wheel again later.'

'That's all right,' she told him. 'You're not late, anyway. You must have intended leaving a lot earlier.'

'Better not to leave anything to chance in this world,' he retorted, and she saw a shadow cross his face.

'Where are we going?' she demanded eagerly.

'I thought we'd drop in at a restaurant I've taken a fancy to, and take a drive later. It's too late to make other arrangements. I don't mind the awkward hours that we work, but it does curtail some of the activities a bit.'

'It's something I shall get used to,' Jane said. 'But I'm very easy to please. I don't mind where I go or what we do.'

He smiled as they got back into the car. He looked almost a different person today, she thought critically as she watched him. They drove away from the farm and took the road to town. Jane relaxed in her seat and prepared to enjoy his company. She had been waiting for this evening. As they sped through the countryside she wondered again if she were unable to fall in love naturally. Why hadn't it happened to her before? Was it that she hadn't met the right man? She recalled the panic she had felt when Steve kissed her. What did it all mean?

She knew that if she started thinking too much about it she might start complexes that would destroy her peace of mind. But it was worrying, all the same. She glanced at Philip, and he was concentrating upon his driving. What would she feel if he kissed her? She smiled at the thought, and studied his mouth and features. Perhaps it wouldn't be so bad. A pang struck through her. A sudden desire lifted in a corner of her mind and she knew the wonder and the agony of desire. But there was a question mark beside it, and Jane didn't like the mixture that brewed itself so deep down inside her.

'Are you settling down in your work?' Philip asked suddenly, glancing at her.

'Yes, thank you. I've never been happier.'

'I can believe you, judging by the expression upon your face at this moment.' He was smiling thinly, and Jane wondered what had happened in his past that set such loneliness upon him.

'I must say that you're looking more cheerful than you were last Sunday,' she ventured. 'Are you beginning to look forward to the future?'

'I am!' He spoke emphatically, and his smile broadened. 'It took a doctor to see what was wrong with me. I expect you're making a great hit with your patients, aren't you?'

'I think I'm doing all right,' Jane said. 'What about you?'

'No complaints so far this week,' he said. 'That's pretty good going for me. I used to get Doctor Wyatt thrust down my throat nearly every day. But my heart wasn't in the practice until last Sunday.'

'Oh?' she demanded innocently. 'And what happened last Sunday?'

'I met someone who taught me a very valuable lesson,' he said. 'I thought I knew all the answers, but I learned differently, and just in time, if I'm any judge at all. I was getting ready to call it a day.'

They were both silent for some time, and Jane watched the countryside as they went through Haylingford and continued. She was thankful that it had happened in time, she was thinking. If he had decided to move away she might never have met him. That would have been a disaster!

'I'm really looking forward to working in the group practice with you,' he said. 'But I doubt if our free time will coincide. Does that mean this will be the first and last time we get out together?'

'I hope not.' Their glances met as she spoke, and Jane had a momentary feeling of pure joy. She relished the emotion because it was so strange to her. It seemed to indicate that she was not as odd as she imagined herself to be.

The restaurant turned out to be an hotel on the outskirts of a neighbouring town, and Jane recalled having been there in the long distant past. They left the car in the park at the rear and went into the hotel. Jane was set to enjoy herself, and it seemed so wonderful to be in Philip's company. She was so enrapt with him that she hardly noticed the meal. There was a three-piece orchestra playing soft music, and Jane slipped into the mood that was being created. The wine Philip had chosen was sweet and rich, and Jane fancied that this was a special occasion for him, although he hadn't admitted as much.

Later, they departed, and Philip took her for a drive, ending up on the coast, parking the car on the cliffs where they could look down at the sea. Night was crawling in across the flat expanse of water, and the evening was peaceful and calm. The breeze that came in at the open windows was cooling, affording relief after the long hours of unrelenting sunshine. Jane closed her eyes and leaned back in her seat.

'This is heavenly,' she said slowly. 'I have the most wonderful feeling that life is going to be excellent from now on.'

'I hope it turns out that way for you.' Philip leaned forward and peered down at the beach below. The shadows were closing in and vision was difficult. 'Are those figures children down there?' he demanded.

Jane jerked herself from her thoughts and peered through the gathering dusk. She nodded as her eyes fixed upon the tiny figures.

'It's hard to tell from up here, but they look too small to be adults or teenagers.'

'They've got a boat or something,' he continued. 'I like messing around in boats, as they say. What about you?'

'I've been on the rivers around Haylingford in a cabin cruiser,' she said. 'I think I might be afraid to try the sea, unless it happened to be like it is now.'

'A fine-weather sailor, eh?' He laughed. 'I'm quite a capable sailor myself. I'd like to take you out when there's a stiff breeze blowing.'

'And if I'm sea-sick?' she demanded.

'I think you'd soon get used to it, and if you took a liking to it you'd always want to be going out.'

'It sounds exciting, but isn't it slightly dangerous?'

'Can you swim?' His face was almost in shadow as their glances met.

'Yes, quite strongly. When I was a schoolgirl I used to swim in a lake on the farm. That was before they got around to building a swimming-pool in Haylingford. I don't have to add that no fish are in the lake now, do I?'

'It's not as bad as that, is it?' he demanded laughingly.

'Father says he'll have to stock it

again,' she retorted. 'Do you like fishing?'

'When I have the time.'

'Then you must come and have some sport. When we start the group you should be able to find more time.'

'Before last Sunday I wouldn't have wanted any spare time,' he mused. 'It's strange how things change, and so suddenly, isn't it? This time last week I didn't know you existed. I had heard about you, of course. Lots of people took great pleasure in telling me that Doctor Ashford's niece was coming to take up a partnership in his practice. They all seemed to think that when you joined your uncle there wouldn't be enough room in the town for me.'

'What a horrible thought!' Jane leaned back and watched his face from under her long lashes. The moon was showing far out over the sea, tracing a widening path of silver magic upon the smooth surface of the water. She began to feel an ethereal magic filling her heart. Desires quickened beneath the surface of her mind, acting secretly as if in league against her. She began to feel strongly aware of his company, and there was an urge inside her to reach out and touch him. She was certain she wouldn't dislike his embrace. She began to hope that before the evening was done he would attempt to kiss her.

'I didn't think I would ever take to Haylingford,' he went on, leaning back and sighing heavily. 'I was beginning to hate the sight of it. But this week I've started getting fond of the place. I've come past your surgery several times when you've been inside. You're the only friend I've got in the town.'

'That's something of an honour, being the only one,' she said. 'Don't you have any friends elsewhere?'

'There were some, but I lost touch with them when I moved.' His voice thickened a little. 'I never had much time for going out and about. I'm something like you in that respect.'

Jane nodded, filled with a hope that they were very similar. As far as she could tell, they had the same tastes. But he seemed cold and remote. Was there any warmth deep inside him, struggling to get out? She wondered what kind of character she presented to him. Was he filled with the same questions?

Darkness slowly closed in, and as they lost their distinctness in the shadows an intimacy gripped Jane. She moved a little closer to him, until their shoulders were touching, and she trembled as she imagined his hands upon her and his mouth against hers. Desire was a physical pain in her breast, and she clenched her hands in her lap and tried to fight off her emotions.

They talked generally, and mostly about what they expected to gain from the group practice. But Jane was experiencing great longing. She was suddenly ripe for love, and wished she had known him much longer. Perhaps he would have unbent a bit if they had been friends for a year or so. She knew she was impatient, and that was surprising.

From time to time Philip glanced at his watch, and Jane wondered what was passing through his mind. Did he want to be getting back to town? Was he bored with her? She froze at the thought, and moistened her lips. She had been afraid of asking him if he wanted to put an end to the evening in case he decided to do so, but she didn't want to put him to any trouble.

'This is the first time I've been able to relax since I came back,' she said slowly. 'You're good company, Philip.'

'Do you think so?' He paused. 'I'm glad. People usually think I'm too quiet.'

'I like a quiet man!' She longed to snuggle up against him. There was a positive ache in her breast. From time to time she breathed deeply in an attempt to control her rising emotions, but it was a losing fight. She almost squirmed in her seat as she tried to keep her imagination from torturing her with impressions of what he would be like in love.

He half-turned towards her suddenly, as if easing a cramped limb. Then his hand went along the back of the seat, and a knuckle touched her neck. Jane tensed, stiffened in every muscle, and she hardly dared to breathe.

'Some people think I'm too quiet,' he said in husky tones. 'I don't think so myself, but there's no telling what's in other people's minds. Quietness can be taken for shyness. I'll bet you think I'm shy.'

'I have considered it,' she replied.

'That's what I thought. But why? Just because I'm quiet? I am enjoying your company. Ought I to make a pass at you just to give you the impression that I'm a bold man in every respect? Some men do that sort of thing because it is expected of them. But I have respect for you, and I'm afraid to do anything that might offend you. It would be dreadful if I lost the only friend I have.'

'There's something in what you say.' Jane forced a gentle laugh, which covered her feelings. She was breathless with anticipation. 'But I'm not so narrow minded that I would take a kiss in a car too seriously.' She was beginning to feel afraid, because she didn't know what her reactions to a kiss would be. She had hated Steve Denny's kiss, had felt revolted even, and that weighed heavily upon her mind. But she wanted Philip to kiss her. She had to know if she was cold towards romance.

'I'm glad you said that, because I've been tormented with the desire to kiss you ever since last Sunday. I'm a very lonely man, Jane, and that's probably the motive behind this desire. But you're not a girl a man could lightly take liberties with. There's something so efficient about you that I feel shrivelled inside.'

'I'm sorry about that.' She smiled. 'Am I to suffer because of my manner? I assure you I am a woman behind the professional mask.'

'I have no doubt of that.' He was moving towards her, and Jane caught her breath as his arm went around her neck, pulling her gently towards him.

This was the moment of truth! She closed her eyes and prayed that she would not be revolted. She clenched her hands and held her breath, and then their lips met and she relaxed and gave herself up to the moment.

For the first moment she felt bewildered, so strong was her desire to enjoy his kiss. Then her instincts went to work, and her arms lifted and circled his neck, pulling him towards her with a strength that was backed by every fibre of her being. A pang struck her and seemed to go right through her. She took a shuddering breath, and clung to him as if her life depended upon it. Time ceased to exist. Nothing else was real in the whole world. This was what she had always hoped for in a kiss. There was sweetness and power combined in his lips, and Jane knew the ecstasy which had so far eluded her.

When they drew apart he was

breathless, and Jane was gasping for breath. They sat with their heads together, their arms around each other, and Jane knew he must have been aware of the emotions that had surged through her. They must have communicated themselves to him.

'Jane,' he whispered. 'I knew the moment I saw you that you would turn out to be very important to me. All this week I've been trying to goad myself into making an approach to you, afraid that I might fail to interest you. There are many other friends in your life, and I feared that you might turn to one of the men. But if I know anything at all about love, then I don't have to worry any longer. You and I are just right for each other.'

'I've just found that out,' she replied in trembling tones. Relief was a strong wave inside her. She had felt completely normal in his arms, with none of the distaste that had come to her in Steve's arms. She felt desire rising in her again, and she turned to him. 'Kiss me again,' she begged, 'just to prove it is true.'

He came to her eagerly, and Jane lost herself in the wonder of their contact. He had the power to move her deeply inside, and that had never happened before, not even when she had believed herself to be in love with Roger all those years before. She clung to him, wanting the moment to last for ever.

'Jane, it's getting late,' he whispered, and she had no idea how long they had been locked in embrace.

'Is it? Does it matter?' she demanded tremulously, and he laughed shakily.

'We have to be on duty tomorrow,' he pointed out. 'Don't get me wrong. I wish we could sit here forever. But time won't halt for anything, and that's a pity. But there will be other times.'

'I sincerely hope so. You're not the only one to feel strongly over the past week.'

'You?' He stared at her, his face just visible in the darkness.

'Me,' she confessed. 'When I saw you last Saturday morning I had a strange feeling about you. That was why I passed by your house on Sunday. I just wanted to see you again.'

'Well I never!' His incredulity was genuine. 'Is it going to be just one of those things between us, Jane? Do you believe in love at first sight?'

'Perhaps not in the way the storybooks have it,' she said slowly, 'but I do think two people can know almost instantly if they are naturally suited to one another. I had that feeling almost at once.'

'It must have been the same thing that came to me,' he said in awe. 'Jane!' His tones thickened with emotion. 'Is it too much to hope that we'll make progress from tonight?'

'I hope not!' She paused, then laughed. 'I mean, I hope it isn't too much to hope for.'

'And I was on the point of throwing up everything and going back to a hospital,' he mused. 'In the past weeks there have been times when I could have contemplated anything but staying here. Now I've met you. You're a life-saver, Jane!'

'I'm very happy about that.' She held his hand tightly. 'I could tell that you were distressed, Philip. It hurt me to see you so unhappy.'

'This time last week I didn't know you existed! Last Saturday morning I cursed that breakdown, but now I can see it was the finest thing that ever happened to me.'

He kissed her again, and time fell into a new habit of making itself timeless. Jane had never felt so moved before. She was quite weak and shaken by the time they drew reluctantly apart. She was boiling inside, and after this evening she would never be the same again. The knowledge was hard and certain inside her. Mingled with it was the relief that she was no different to other girls. When she met the right man, she knew it and acted accordingly.

'We'd better go, Jane,' he said, an edge of his mind fixed in reality. 'I don't want to get you home too late in case your parents object. I wouldn't want anything to mar this evening. It will live in my mind until I die.'

She nodded, unable to speak. Her throat was constricted and she felt as if she were floating in a pool of ecstasy.

'So much is happening this week,' he continued as he switched on the engine. 'Jane, can this all really be happening?'

'If it is a dream,' she whispered, 'then I hope I shall never wake up.'

He leaned across and kissed her gently, and she quivered with deep feeling. She was shaken to the core, and it was a wonderful feeling. But there were strange thoughts flooding her mind. This revelation opened up new horizons for her. She sat silently at his side as he drove homeward, and her mind was inundated with conjecture. She took hold of his arm, holding it gently to avoid interfering with his driving, and he turned his head and kissed her cheek. Words were not necessary now. She knew it as she gazed at him.

So this was why she had returned home! He had been here waiting for her, although he hadn't known it, and Fate had wasted no time in throwing them together. But it was up to them to work out the rest of it, and Jane knew they would have a wonderful time doing just that. Love was rearing its head after sleeping in her breast from the day she was born. She knew it was love. The real thing couldn't be more poignant, any sharper. This was the apex of her feelings, and she knew life would never seem the same again after. Her fortunes were riding the crest of the wave, and she felt that it would go on forever!

7

In the days that followed, Jane was sublimely happy. Work went off without a hitch, and nothing was too much trouble for her. Time had lost its essential element. She seemed beyond the touch of reality. When she looked at her reflection in the mirror she almost failed to recognise the starry-eyed girl who looked back at her. She wondered if others could see the changes in her, but dared not broach the subject even to her mother. She was afraid that talking about it would shatter the illusions that filled her. Nothing could be permitted to harm the sweet dreams building up in her mind.

Philip, too, seemed a different man. He smiled more frequently, and always seemed to be meeting her. Even when she did the country round she saw him. His car was always ahead of her, and each time she set eyes upon him her heart would leap and her pulses raced.

As time went by they became more comfortable with one another. Each day found her learning something new about him, and she disliked nothing that formed in her mind. Physically he was exactly what she had dreamed of in a man, and he kept telling her in his quiet way that she filled the bill as far as he was concerned. She was enthusiastic in her approach to loving him. She had never been in love before. There was confidence in each of them, and time could only cement the feeling which had sprung up between them.

But there was more to Jane's life than Philip and their love. The whole subject was never very far from the surface of her mind, but duty was a harsh mistress, and the days followed one another busily into the past. Jane began to feel that she was living on a merry-go-round. There was never any sense of stopping, of being able to sit down and think clearly over what was happening. If she wasn't in the surgery listening to the symptoms of her patients, then she was driving around the town or the villages making calls at the houses of the patients. It was a fast pace, and never ending, but it suited her. She felt that she had to keep on the move because her happiness was a living thing inside and needed to be pushed on towards the inevitable end. But she dared not consider what that end might be.

The logical and natural end ought to be love and marriage. But she could not envisage herself as a wife. They were both doctors, and their lives would be wrapped around their work. There would have to be a lot of give and take in such a marriage. Could it really work? She knew she would try hard enough to make it do so, but there would be difficult times for the both of them.

She saw nothing of Steve Denny after that evening when he had kissed her and she rebuked him. Perhaps he was smarting from the blows to his love and pride. She was relieved that he hadn't come back again, although she hoped that he was not too badly hurt. She could imagine what his feelings were, and she sympathised because she knew what a blow it would be to her if Philip decided that he didn't love her.

But there were no fears of that. When they met now Philip showed his feelings. It took several weeks for him to come to the point where he could take her into his arms with complete freedom from shyness, but when he did his manner changed and he never stopped telling her how much he loved her.

Jane was content. This was what life was all about. Love was the fulfilment, the ultimate goal of most men and women. Until it came, there was a sense of something lacking, a restless feeling that the search had to go on. Some people were unfortunate in that they never found their true love. But Jane had no doubts. Philip was all she wanted out of life.

Four weeks after they had agreed to start a group practice, Philip moved into his new surgery opposite Jane's. His patients came to see him, or Jane and her uncle, depending upon their duties, and they found more free time. Instead of being on duty in the evenings every other night, or every night in Philip's case, they were on call only one night in three. The daily duties were split into three parts, and there was plenty of free time for each of them. It gave Jane and Philip time enough to spend hours together. They went out in his car, and spent long hours sitting and talking about their work and the future.

July turned into August, and August ran its course. When Jane was off duty there was no one else in the world but Philip. He was a frequent visitor to the farm, and at weekends when they were free they were never out of each other's company.

Jane saw little of her friends as the weeks went by. From time to time she called at Dorothy Beck's hairdressing salon, and learned more about her large circle of friends, but she seemed to be out of step with them. Her mind was too occupied with Philip for anyone to be able to intrude into her life, and even Roger Keeble gave up trying to see her after the first few attempts failed. She learned that Steve was still going around as usual, but he was drinking more, and drifting away from his regular haunts and friends.

Reality seemed far away from Jane. Her life was so happy that it didn't seem true. It was like living a dream, but there was the advantage of knowing that she would never wake up and find it all gone. The security that came to her with the knowledge uplifted her. Everything she did had the backing of pure confidence, and she succeeded all the more because of it.

Then she found Steve Denny's name on her list one morning, and when she called at his house his mother showed a worried face at the door.

'Jane, I'm so glad it's you and not your uncle,' Mrs Denny said. 'I've had a rare old time trying to get Steve to stay in bed to see the doctor, and he threatened to lock the door of his room if you came. But this morning he is really ill. He couldn't get up if he tried.'

'What's the matter with him?' Jane demanded, stepping across the threshold.

'The root of it all is his drinking,' Mrs Denny told her worriedly. 'I don't know what's come over him lately, Jane, but he's drinking far too much, and it's no use talking to him. I might just as well try to communicate with a brick wall.'

'Well, let me visit him and see what we can do,' Jane said firmly. She followed the woman up to a bedroom, and was shocked when she saw Steve's face. He was propped up on a pillow, looking very sick indeed, and there was such a hang-dog air about him that she felt a pang inside as she wondered if she were the cause of his illness. She took a deep breath as she set down her bag. 'Hello, Steve,' she said, 'what seems to be the trouble?'

'I don't need a doctor,' he retorted ungraciously. 'I told you not to send for anyone, Mother.'

'Well, I'm here now, and you certainly look as if you need some medical attention.' Jane spoke firmly, in her no-nonsense voice, and he blinked and turned his head away. 'Do you have any pain anywhere?' she demanded.

'No. I just feel in the need of a rest,' he replied. 'It's nothing to worry about. I've been working rather hard lately, and it's been a bit too much, I expect.'

'You've been slacking at work and drinking too much, Steve,' Mrs Denny said. 'Tell Jane all about it. She'll help you, if anyone can.'

'She's helped me already,' he replied heavily, closing his eyes. 'But there's nothing she can do for me. Just go away and leave me alone.'

'Put out your tongue,' Jane commanded, going to his side. She waited until he complied reluctantly. Then she took his pulse and temperature. 'What about pains?' she demanded.

'None,' he retorted. 'Mother told you what the trouble is. I have been drinking too much, but that's not reason enough to see a doctor.'

'But if it is affecting your health, then why drink so much?' Jane demanded. 'It's rather silly, isn't it?'

'What else is there to do in this stupid town?' His dark eyes glowered at her.

Jane sighed. She considered him for a moment, then nodded slowly. 'There's nothing wrong with you that a week in bed wouldn't cure,' she said. 'Rest and complete abstention from drinking alcohol. I'll write a prescription for some tablets, and you're to take three a day, after meals. I'll call in and see you in two days.'

'I don't want any medicine,' he retorted. 'I'll be up tomorrow. I've got to get back to work.'

'You'll see that he complies with my

instructions, Mrs Denny?' Jane turned to his mother.

'I'll do my best, but he's past the stage where I can make him mind. I'll get his father to try and talk some sense into him, but Steve is old enough to know better now.'

'Goodbye, Steve.' Jane handed the scribbled prescription to Mrs Denny. 'Do as you're told, won't you?' Her tones suggested she was addressing a wayward schoolboy. 'Stay in bed until I call again. If you don't heed my orders you're likely to finish up being really ill. You're not that foolish, are you?'

'I'm not in the least concerned about what might happen to me,' he declared, and turned his back upon her.

Jane departed, and stood by the front door with Mrs Denny. They talked about Steve, and Jane felt awful as she listened to the woman's worries. She had the feeling that Steve was drinking too much because she had rejected him. But that was absurd! Surely he hadn't fallen in love with her since her return! But she thought of the time it had taken her to realise that she was in love with Philip, and she knew time didn't enter into it. If Steve was in love with her, then he was having a dreadful time trying to get over it. But she felt helpless about the situation. There was nothing she could do to help him. Anything she did in that respect could only make matters worse.

'I'm so worried about him because he's never been like this before, Jane,' Mrs Denny said. 'Steve has always been a hard-working boy. He seemed quite happy that you were coming back to town, but that was weeks ago, and something has happened to upset him. I think he's fallen in love with someone and it hasn't worked out.'

Jane was sure of it, but didn't say so. She suppressed a sigh as she replied.

'It happens to everyone at some time in life, Mrs Denny, and Steve must learn to face up to it. Anyway, give him those tablets, and I'll call again the day after tomorrow. Perhaps it would be better if I had my uncle stop by to see him.'

'It might at that,' Mrs Denny said. 'I'm sorry Steve wasn't more co-operative, Jane. But perhaps he felt shy because it was you calling.'

'I don't think that worried him,' Jane replied, and took her leave. She was thoughtful as she went on with her round. She felt responsible for what was happening to Steve, although he ought to have faced up to it with more strength of character.

She always arranged her route to enable herself to be in the region of home for lunch, and just after twelve she arrived at the farm to find Philip there, talking to her mother.

'Hello,' Jane queried with a smile. 'Loafing around on your day off?'

'There's nothing quite like it,' he retorted. 'But actually I've come out to take advantage of your father's offer of some fishing. Do you remember that I told you I never had the time to avail myself of pursuits like that?'

'I do indeed!' Jane's dark eyes sparkled as she regarded him. 'So you're finding life has become easier since joining the group?'

'Very much easier.' His blue eyes told her more than his words. 'I feel like a totally different man.'

Mrs Ashford broke into their talk. 'I'll tell Mrs Gartside you're home, Jane. Philip is having lunch with us, and he'll be here for tea. You're taking surgery tonight, aren't you?'

'Yes, this is my busy day,' Jane admitted. 'It's a pity we can't arrange to have our days off together, Philip.'

'We do all right at the weekends,' he retorted.

'That's true, but, like most women, I'm never satisfied.' Jane laughed musically as she went to wash up, and when she returned to the dining-room her father had come in.

Philip had fitted in with her family as if he had been made for them, Jane realised as she watched him through the meal. She was under the impression that Fate had arranged all of this, that Philip was the most suitable man alive for her. The more she learned about him, the better she understood this. Now she could hardly remember what life without him was like.

After the meal she saw him out to the lake, and stayed with him far longer than she ought to have done. Only when he ordered her to go back to work did she push up her face for a kiss and then turn away. But she had hardly gone six paces before he caught up with her and took her into his arms.

'Jane, the more I see you the more I love you,' he said softly. 'I can never quite believe my luck in finding you. I can honestly say that there's nothing about you I don't like. I've looked for faults and can find none. If you have any, then you're keeping them extremely well hidden.'

'Shall I say the same about you?' she demanded, her eyes sparkling.

'I doubt if you can, and I wouldn't want you to lie,' he retorted with a grin.

'I wouldn't lie, and I can repeat your words without fear of exaggerating anything. I suppose you know that my life is revolving around you now.'

'I'm sure of it.' He raised her chin with a gentle hand. 'I would have to be blind not to notice, Jane. How long have we known each other now?'

'Six weeks?' she queried, then nodded. 'This is the sixth week. What do you really think of me, Philip?'

'I love you more than anything in the world, so I'm biased, aren't I? How can I answer that question when everything in my mind is coloured and conditioned by you?'

'Are you sorry for the way things are turning out?'

'How are they turning out?' he queried with a grin.

'I don't know how it seems to you, but I have definite opinions on that subject.' Her eyes sparkled. 'But I really must go now, Philip. Don't fall in, will you?'

'I can swim,' he retorted.

'I know, but I was thinking of the fish,' she replied.

He drew her tightly into his arms and kissed her soundly. Jane closed her eyes and let her thoughts and impressions have full sway. When he released her she overbalanced, and he caught her with steady hands.

'That's the kind of effect you have upon me,' she said lightly, and took her leave of him.

During the afternoon her thoughts returned to Philip on more than one occasion. He was settling down well, and the loneliness which had beset him before her return was now a thing of the past. But her mind was trying to take the next step in their lives before she or he was ready to admit to it. They had admitted to one another that love filled them. How long would it be before Philip asked her to marry him?

The subject was on the surface of her mind for some time, and she wondered what her answer would be to his proposal. Would she accept? For some reason the answer failed to materialise, and that concerned her. But speculation was not one of her habits, and when she finished her round back in Haylingford she went to the surgery.

John was on duty in the surgery, and there was one patient in his waiting-room. When the patient had gone, Jane went in to see her uncle, and he greeted her warmly.

'Just finished?' he demanded. 'So have I.'

'I'll be here from five-thirty,' Jane said. 'I'm on my way home now, John.'

'What sort of a day has it been for you?'

'Agreeable. The weather is right for driving around.'

'Any problems?' he demanded.

'Only one, but it really isn't a problem of ours,' she replied. 'I saw Steve Denny this morning. He's been drinking heavily lately and his stomach is protesting, rather sharply, I'd say, judging by the looks of him. He isn't seriously ill, and if he follows my instructions he'll be all right in a day or two.'

'So what's the problem, Jane?' John demanded. He got up from his desk and began to pace the room.

'I think he's taken to drink because I refused to have anything to do with him,' she said. 'So it's no use my seeing him. I was thinking perhaps it would be better if you called on him tomorrow. I said I'd drop in again in two days.'

'What do you want me to say to him?' John queried, pausing by the window to turn and regard her seriously.

'I don't know!' Jane shook her head. 'I feel responsible for his condition, that's all.'

'If your reason is correct, then the only way you can help him is by becoming his girl-friend or something, isn't it?'

'That's a rather drastic treatment, don't you think?'

'Only if you don't care for him, and I suppose that is the reason why you refuse to have anything to do with him.' He watched her face for a moment, nodding slowly. 'Jane, the only advice I can give to you is don't become personally involved with the patients. Treat their ailments and leave it at that.'

'That's exactly what I am doing,' she pointed out.

'Good. You can cure 'most anything they come here with, but you can't eliminate the causes, whether it's flu or tonsillitis. The same goes for the sort of thing you've just outlined. If Steve Denny wants to drink himself to death, then there's nothing you can do about it, apart from warning him of the consequences of his actions. Once you have done that, there's nothing else. So don't worry about it, Jane. I know the tendency is to try and do too much, but the patients don't expect anything more than a few competent words and some medicine. They will even resent a few observations on the way they lead their lives.'

'I know, but Steve is a friend.'

'When a doctor is on duty he has no friends,' John retorted with a grim smile. 'Always bear that in mind, Jane.' He watched her for a few moments. 'I'll drop in and see Steve tomorrow, so forget about it, but let's touch another subject now, shall we?'

'What's that?'

'You and Philip!'

Jane smiled. 'What do you want to know?'

'I really suggested this group practice business in the first place because I thought you and Philip would make a good pair together.' John smiled as he watched her face for reaction.

'You old match-maker!' It was Jane's turn to smile. 'So you were designing all the time.'

'Not to the extent that you're thinking,' he replied unashamedly. 'I thought Nature would do the rest once I got you together. I haven't been far wrong, have I?'

'No. Things are working out perfectly.' Jane did not prevent her eyes taking on a sparkle. She knew she could hide nothing from John. 'I'm very happy with the way things are shaping.'

'And so am I. You two are spending quite a lot of time together. What kind of a man is he? I know he's one of the best professionally. I can't fault his work, and I must say the same about you. Your training has been first class, Jane. You're a great asset in this practice.'

'Thank you for saying so.' She was happy with his praise. 'I don't have to point out to you that you've done a great deal for me, and for Philip. You had nothing to gain from this group practice, did you?'

'Yes I did!' He nodded emphatically. 'I've got satisfaction in a job well done. You don't know what it means to me to see your name on the door, and to know that you are here only because I wanted it so.'

'Why did you never marry, John?' she demanded. 'Or is it too personal a question?'

'Not at all. It's quite simple, really. I never met the right woman. I had firm ideas on the girl I wanted, but she never walked into my life. Haylingford is still a quiet backwater of life, you know, but in my young days it was the back of the beyond.'

'Don't you regret it sometimes?' Jane wanted to know. 'You wanted me to be a boy. Wouldn't it have been better if you'd had a son?'

'It's too late for me to look back on my life and discover that,' he replied. 'Things could have been different, and perhaps they ought to have been. But I'm well satisfied with the place as it is now. You keep on as you're doing and I'll never have cause to complain. I'm very happy, Jane.'

'I'm so glad, John. My life has opened up considerably since I've been back. But, whatever happens, I want you to be satisfied with all the work that's gone into making me a doctor.'

'What happens if you decide to marry?' he demanded.

'I shall remain a doctor in practice,' Jane replied. 'I don't think it will make any difference to that side of my life.'

'Good.' He came forward and patted her shoulder. 'Now you'd better be on your way if you're coming back here at five-thirty. I won't stay a minute after my time, and your patients will be queueing up to see you.'

'I'll be on time, John,' she murmured happily. 'When are you coming out to the farm again?'

'My day off tomorrow!' He nodded slowly. 'I think I'll try some of your father's fishing, if Philip hasn't caught them all today.'

'And you'll drop in and see Steve Denny tomorrow?'

'On my way out to your place to do some fishing,' he declared.

Jane went home, satisfied that she had done all she could for Steve. But her mind was not completely easy about him as she drove up to the farm. She parked the car and went to see if Philip was still at the lake, and he was.

He had half a dozen small fish in his keepnet, and Jane watched him as she approached, for he was so absorbed in fishing that he didn't hear her. When she bent to kiss the back of his neck he almost fell into the water, and turned quickly to her.

'Jane, I didn't hear you! What's the time?' He glanced at his watch. 'Good Lord! I lost all sense of time.'

'That's why you get a day off,' she said, squatting down at his side. 'No need to ask if you have enjoyed yourself today. It's written all over your face.'

'What shall we do this evening?' he demanded, putting an arm around her neck.

'I won't finish at the surgery until seven. But after that my time is yours.'

He looked down at her. Jane watched his face. He was so handsome, she thought, and so unselfish. He had exactly the right temperament for her. It was strange how they had come together, and everything was working out right. It was more than she could ever have hoped for.

'You're a wonderful girl,' he remarked.

'I shall be getting big-headed if you don't tone down that sort of talk,' she told him lightly. 'John was saying something quite like it this afternoon while we were talking. It seems I can do no wrong.'

'Then I agree implicitly with him,' he retorted. 'But tell me one thing, Jane.'

'Anything, and gladly,' she said.

'Do you believe in long engagements?' He was smiling, but intent upon her answer, and Jane suddenly felt at a loss for words. Marriage was the next logical step, but she just could not bring her mind to focus upon it.

'I've never really given it any thought,' she said slowly, her face changing. 'What about you?'

'Me neither,' he retorted, 'but I'm beginning to think that perhaps we ought to consider it. That special finger on your left hand looks rather bare, don't you agree?'

Jane lifted up the hand in question

and stared at it as if she had never seen it before. But she nodded slowly, filled with a query that seemed to envelop her completely.

'I think I do agree,' she said, and he reached down and lifted her gently to her feet.

'Then let me get it off my chest before my nerve fails me,' he told her, staring deeply into her eyes. 'You know that I love you, Jane, and I know you love me. Will you marry me?'

'Yes, Philip!' The words came from her heart without thought, and her mind was kind enough not to thrust up those doubts which she secretly held. He kissed her hungrily, and Jane let go her last hold on reality.

8

Jane found her happiness deepening in the following days. At the first opportunity Philip took her along to the jeweller's and she chose a beautiful engagement ring, a cluster of tiny diamonds set upon a shoulder of platinum, and for some hours afterwards she could not take her eyes off the glinting proof of Philip's love. He took her out to dinner that night, and they danced until very late. It was like entering a dream world, and Jane was blissfully happy. Life seemed to take on a note of unreality as she went about her daily duties, her mind struggling to concentrate upon her work while every impulse was pointed towards the happiness and joy that lay in her future. Nowhere was there a sour note, and she was thankful to the fates for such fortunate treatment. She didn't think any girl could have been so happy as she.

The routine of general practice settled upon her easily, and she was soon working without thought to the fears that had attended her first days. Now she was proving her worth, and the knowledge that she was added to her enjoyment of life.

Calling into Dorothy's hairdressing salon one afternoon for a wash and set, Jane was upset to learn that Steve Denny had gone away. Dorothy was full of it, and after chatting about Jane's engagement the girl launched into an account of the troubles that had come to Steve. Jane made no comment, feeling that she was to blame more than a little for what was happening to Steve.

'His mother was in yesterday afternoon, Jane,' Dorothy went on. 'It seems Steve is in love with some girl who doesn't want to know, and he's really cut up about it. You attended him when he was ill not long ago, didn't you?'

'Yes. There was nothing seriously

wrong. Just too much drink. But he never used to drink like that.' Jane could feel guilt inside her as she spoke. It was her fault, although she couldn't be blamed for being unable to reciprocate Steve's love. That sort of thing happened to a lot of men, and most of them managed to grin and bear it. But there were weaknesses in Steve's make-up, and strain had made them apparent. All Jane could do was hope that he'd get over it fairly quickly.

'He's pulled out of his father's business, Jane, and is going to set up by himself in some other place. Of course, his mother is upset, and I'd think his father is, too. Steve is the only child. His father has worked long and hard to build up the business for Steve.'

'Any idea who this unknown girl is that he's in love with?' Jane asked casually.

'Even Mrs Denny doesn't know,' Dorothy retorted. 'I've been talking to Kay about it, and Kay gets a lot of information on what's happening around and about, but she doesn't know. The only thing we've come up with is that Steve seemed to go to pieces when you arrived back here, Jane.'

'Well, that must be a coincidence,' Jane said, forcing a smile. 'Steve and I were never more than friends.'

'And you've got Philip Carson,' Dorothy said enviously. 'I wish I could find someone like him! But I don't suppose I shall ever get married now. There's no one around who appeals. Kay feels the same way.'

'Do you go out to meet people?' Jane demanded.

'Some people don't have to go out to meet people,' Dorothy retorted. 'But some people are lucky, aren't they?'

'I've certainly had more than my share of good fortune since I've been back,' Jane admitted. 'I feel as if I've been on a merry-go-round from the moment I came home.'

'After being away all those years, you came back at the right time to meet

Doctor Carson.' Dorothy nodded. 'But it couldn't have happened to a nicer girl, Jane. You deserve someone like him. I hope you'll both be very happy.' She paused. 'Have you set the date yet?'

'Not yet. But there's plenty of time. Of course, you'll be invited, Dorothy, and Kay will get the orders for the dresses.' Jane felt her face flush with pleasure as she spoke. It still didn't seem quite real to her. Sometimes, when she thought of Philip and all that he had come to mean to her, she couldn't take it all in, and the sheer happiness was almost too much for her. But it was no dream, and she had the memories of Philip's arms and kisses to impress her with the reality.

'I suppose it will be a spring wedding,' Dorothy continued. 'The end of March or the beginning of April. But will you carry on with your work, Jane?'

'I wouldn't want to give it up,' Jane replied. 'At the moment I wouldn't be able to, even if I wanted. There's too much for just two doctors.'

'But what about when you get married? You and Philip will go away, won't you? Can your uncle run the practice without the both of you?'

'No. We'll probably get in a locum, or two, until we return.' Jane took a deep breath as the prospect of getting married sent a pang through her. She wondered, as she settled back and listened to Dorothy's chatter, just when they would get around to naming the day. Would they wait until they really knew one another? She felt that she knew Philip quite well enough right now. She couldn't love him more! She knew without doubt that he was the man for her. But he had to be certain for himself, and Jane had no desire to hurry him into a decision. When he thought the time was ripe, then he would tell her.

Meeting Philip later, she went with him to his home, and when they were inside the large house he faced her. Jane watched his features. She never tired of looking at him. He smiled and took her into his arms. After he had kissed her he held her at arm's length.

'There's a lot to do, Jane,' he said. 'Time is awasting, as they used to say. We've got to start putting this house in order.' He paused and studied her intent face. 'I'm taking it for granted that you will want to live here with me after we're married! But I ought to ask first. Would you care to live here or do you prefer a modern place? What about a bungalow? We don't need such a large place because we're not having the surgery and waiting-room here.' He pulled a face as he considered her. 'What do you say, Jane?'

'I don't mind where we live, Philip,' she replied eagerly. 'I leave it entirely up to you.'

'Let's have a look around.' He took her hand and led her through the rooms. They went upstairs and looked around, and Jane thought the house was much too large for comfort.

'I think we'll settle for a new bungalow,' Philip said slowly. 'My wife deserves something better than this. Shall we start looking around, dearest?'

'Yes.' Jane was certain they ought to start making plans for the future.

'Three bedrooms ought to be enough for us,' he mused. 'You'll keep working after we're married, Jane?'

'Of course,' she said promptly, and he smiled and kissed her. 'But with all these preparations about to start, are you planning to set a date?'

'It's been in the back of my mind for several days,' he admitted. 'What about late March?'

'That sounds fine. We'll need to think of getting a locum to take over here with Uncle while we're away.'

'There is so much to think of,' he admitted. 'Let's look at a calendar and see if we can't fix a date.'

Jane was light-headed with happiness as they went down to his study. He sat down at his desk and Jane leaned over him as he went through his desk diary for next year's calendar.

'Here we are,' he announced. 'Now

to look at March. The tenth is on a Saturday. I suppose that will be the best day of the week to choose because there's no evening surgery.'

'Then let's settle for the tenth,' Jane said huskily.

He got to his feet and took her into his arms. Jane closed her eyes. He kissed her and she clung to him, her mind filled with a riot of happy thoughts.

'So it'll be the tenth of March, next year,' he mused. 'That date will be the most important one in my life, Jane.'

'Me, too!' she whispered. 'Shall we announce it now?'

'The sooner the better, and we'd better find the time to draw up a list of the things that must be done. We're both of us so wrapped up in our work that anything might be forgotten. I'll remember all the obvious things, like the ring, but there must be a host of other details that I have no inkling about.'

'I'll put Mother to work on them,

and she'll see that nothing is over-looked,' Jane said.

'We'll get the bungalow just after Christmas, shall we?' he demanded. 'Then you can furnish it at your leisure. I hope you have good colour sense and whatnot, because I'm pretty hopeless at that sort of thing.'

Jane kissed him enthusiastically. He smiled at her delight, and nodded slowly.

'You're sure you're doing the right thing, Jane?' he asked. 'You say you love me, but are you pretty sure in your own mind that you can marry me and live happily ever after?'

'Yes, Philip,' she replied, holding herself close to him and pressing her face into his shoulder. 'What about you?'

'Me?' He smiled as he stared down at her. 'You don't have to question me, dearest. I love you. I've been looking for you all my life. Now that I've found you I shan't ever let you go.'

'I sometimes find that I can hardly

believe all of this,' Jane said. 'I'm half-afraid that one day I shall wake up and find it's all been a dream.'

'That's how I feel about you,' he admitted with a smile. 'So we both have it very bad, Jane. That's a relief to know. But we're not doing so badly, you know. We haven't known each other very long in terms of time. We've come together very quickly. So we can count our blessings. We've found in a matter of weeks what it takes some people half a lifetime to discover.'

Jane nodded. She was more than content. Now they had a definite date to work towards she knew exactly where she stood . . .

Life went on with a seemingly increasing tempo. One day followed another in fast succession. Attending the surgery or handling the country round made no impression upon the fleeting hours. Summer faded and the climate changed imperceptibly. The countryside always showed depression when the leaves started falling and the flowers died. But this year Jane didn't seem to notice the signs. Her mind was firmly fixed upon next spring.

When she received a call from Mrs Denny one morning, asking for her to call, Jane felt a pang of premonition. She agreed to call when the surgery was over, and spent the rest of the time wondering if something had happened to Steve. There had been little talk of Steve since he left home, and the silence surrounding him had made Jane think that he had forgotten about her and was settling down in his new surroundings. With her last patient leaving the office, she felt able to depart, and set off quickly for the Denny house.

Mrs Denny admitted her, and Jane felt her fears quicken when she saw the woman's face.

'Aren't you well, Mrs Denny?' she demanded.

'I'm only worried,' came the reply. 'It's so good of you to come, Jane. I know you must be terribly busy, but it's about Steve.'

Jane nodded. She had guessed as much. 'What's the trouble?' she demanded.

'He came home early this morning, and he looks dreadful,' Mrs Denny continued. 'I'm sure he hasn't taken care of himself properly, and his drinking is as bad. He's swallowed half a bottle of sherry since he's been here.'

'Is he ill?' Jane demanded. 'I mean, does he need a doctor?'

'I think he does, but he won't listen. What am I going to do with him, Jane? I had to call you because you and Steve are good friends. I thought you might know how to reach him. No amount of talking on my part will do any good.'

'I'm sorry to hear this, Mrs Denny, but there's little I can do. I'll speak to Steve, if you really want me to, but he has every right to tell me to mind my own business. Apart from that, I think I'm the cause of Steve's trouble.'

'You, Jane!' Mrs Denny stared at her in disbelief. 'What on earth do you mean?'

Jane slowly explained the incident

out at the farm when Steve had kissed her, and Mrs Denny's face showed agony.

'So that's it,' the woman said slowly. 'And you're getting married to Doctor Carson early next year, aren't you?'

'I am. I'm so sorry about Steve. He was one of the nicest men I've ever known, but he wasn't the man for me. I suspect that he's taken it hard. I had hoped he would have got over it by now.'

'Don't blame yourself, Jane!' Mrs Denny touched her hand. 'I did have my suspicions, as a matter of fact, but Steve would never tell me anything. That's the way of the world, isn't it? But perhaps you'd better not see him, if that is the cause of his trouble. It might only upset him. And I was looking to you for help and support.' She shook her head slowly. 'This has ruined him, Jane! His father has given him up for lost, and there's no helping him. What shall I do?'

'There's nothing anyone can do,

except hope that he'll snap out of it before his health is impaired,' Jane said. 'I'm most dreadfully sorry, Mrs Denny, I really am!'

'I'll do what I can for him,' the woman went on. 'If I use understanding perhaps he'll respond. I'm sorry I bothered you, Jane. But I'm certain it will do more harm than good if you saw him now.'

'What are his plans?' Jane demanded. 'Is he remaining at home now?'

'I don't know yet. All he's told me is that he's spent an awful lot of money, and the business he tried to start with some partner has come unstuck. I don't know what his father will say, I'm sure. I dread to contemplate their meeting.'

Jane took her leave, filled with anxiety. No matter what way she looked at it, the blame seemed to rest with her. She went home to lunch, her mind preoccupied with the problem, and what was so galling was the fact that there was nothing she could do.

Anything she tried could only make matters worse.

After lunch she was free until evening surgery at five-thirty. Philip was on duty now, handling appointments made during the day. With nothing to do, Jane decided to go for a tramp across the fields, and pulled on a pair of Wellingtons and wrapped up against the wind that cut across the bare landscape. She felt she had a lot to think out, but there were no problems, just details that had to be straightened.

Generally, she was happy with the way her life had worked out. She strode out across the meadow beyond the farmhouse and found the cart track that meandered through the fields. This was familiar territory to her, but had not known her footprints for quite a long time. She gazed around with eyes that saw everything anew, and it was good to recall sights that had been buried by other impressions from later years. She found it difficult to get her mind to work on what she wanted, but it didn't matter. Time would iron out anything that needed attention.

When she reached the limit of her father's fields in this direction she halted and stared away across the countryside. There were so many fields, and all of them were used at some time or other. She liked to stand alone and think back across the years, past the time when she was born, to the generations who had been before. She was a romantic, she knew, and her imagination weaved strange thoughts of what life must have been like for those vague people who had inherited the earth so long before. Then there was a shifting of outlook, and she tried to imagine the earth as it would be when her generation had gone the way of all the others before it. What would life be like in a hundred or two hundred years ahead?

It made her realise that life was so short. Everything seemed to fit into perspective, and it served to illuminate the fact that she was just a very insignificant speck in the scheme of things. Jane shivered as she turned back. The loneliness of the afternoon affected her deeply; made her feel as if she had been holding silent communion with unknown powers. But it was good for her soul, and she felt fresh inside as she retraced her steps.

There was so much to look forward to in the future. The knowledge was firm, like a shining goal ahead of her. She hadn't known this great joy lay waiting for her when she returned to take up her part in John's practice. Now it was unfolding like some wonderful romantic story. The pleasure exceeded her wildest hopes. She had thought of her future sometimes, wondering if she would ever meet a man she could love, and he had been here all the time, just waiting for her to arrive.

By the time she reached the farmhouse her legs ached and she was tired, but the air had put colour into her cheeks and she felt hungry. There was just time for tea before she had to go to the surgery, and she changed slowly and then went down to find her mother.

'There's been a call for you, Jane,' Mrs Ashford said. 'It was nothing important, or I would have come looking for you. Mrs Denny wants to see you again, and I told her you'd be in your surgery between five-thirty and seven.'

'Did she say what was wrong?' Jane demanded.

'No. She'll call on you at the surgery.' Mrs Ashford took in Jane's flushed cheeks. 'That outing this afternoon did you good. I wish I had felt up to the exercise myself. Many's the time I've walked across those fields, taking you with me, when you were a child.'

'I can remember some of the occasions,' Jane replied with a smile. 'It's wonderful to get right out there all alone. It seems to bring home the solid truths of our existence.'

'That's exactly how it used to make me feel.' Mrs Ashford smiled as if they were sharing a secret. 'I always took that walk if I had some problem to solve.' She paused. 'Was there something on your mind, Jane?'

'No!' Jane shook her head. 'At least, I'm not aware of anything. I didn't have to think over anything. Of course, there are a lot of things on my mind. The wedding is drawing nearer, although it is still some months away, but, with Christmas over, the weeks will fly. You'll be a great help, Mother.'

'It will be strange having you married and out of the house.' There was a wistful note in Mrs Ashford's voice, and Jane went to her mother's side.

'I shall always be around, Mother,' she said. 'But I do see what you mean.'

'I'm happy for you, Jane. You deserve someone like Philip. I wouldn't have chosen anyone else if the choice for you had been mine. I'm so glad you're happy about it.'

'I can't believe my own luck,' Jane retorted. 'Everything happened at once, as soon as I returned, and it will take some getting used to.'

'That's how life ought to work out,' her mother said. 'But we mustn't let the time get away from us. You'd better start writing out a list of the people you want to attend the wedding. Has Philip given you any idea of his side?'

'Not yet! I do know he has no immediate family; no brothers or sisters, but there are sure to be others. I'll have a word with him about that. When I've got time I'll drop in to see Kay at the dress shop. It's better to start the preparations too soon than to leave them too late. But I get the feeling sometimes that it's all a dream, that I'll be wasting my time starting all the arrangements.'

'It will strike you like that, and towards the end you may wish you'd said no when Philip asked you to marry him, but that will pass, and afterwards you'll be very happy, Jane.'

'I hope so. It must be dreadful to make a mistake in that part of life.'

'You don't have any doubts, do you?'

There was a note of anxiety in Mrs Ashford's voice, and Jane quickly shook her head.

'No! Don't get me wrong, Mother! It isn't that at all. It's just that I have to get used to the idea. I'm overjoyed with life as it is.'

Her mother nodded wisely. 'Those doubts are only natural,' she explained. 'But don't keep anything to yourself, Jane. If you do have any problems, then tell me about them, won't you?'

'You can be sure that I will,' Jane said, smiling. She hugged her mother, and kissed her cheek. 'Now I'd better forget all that for now and concentrate upon more mundane things. If I don't hurry I shall be late at the surgery.'

She was thoughtful as she drove into Haylingford. Her mind was now back in its day-to-day elevation, and she reminded herself of what lay before her as she went into the surgery. She was on time, and started work upon arrival. It was better to be slightly ahead than behind. But she had forgotten Mrs

Denny until Milly called her on the telephone to say Mrs Denny had arrived and would like to see her when it was convenient. Jane finished with a patient and went out to the waiting-room. One look at Mrs Denny's face was enough to warn her that something was seriously wrong.

'Come in, Mrs Denny,' she said as the woman got to her feet.

'I'm so sorry to trouble you at a time like this,' came the apologetic reply. 'But I must talk to you, Jane.'

They went into the office and Jane pulled forward a chair. Mrs Denny sank into it and covered her face with her hands. Jane stared at her for some moments, filled with strange omens that made her uneasy.

'It's about Steve you've called, isn't it, Mrs Denny?'

'Yes!' The woman lowered her hands and sat up straight. 'Jane, I'm at my wits' end! I just don't know what to do any more.'

'Tell me about it.' Jane sat down

behind her desk and leaned her arms upon it, clasping her hands together. 'I have a few moments to spare before I see the next patient. What's happened?'

'Steve went out at lunch time, and heard that you're going to get married in the spring. He came home the worse for drink, and when I got on to him about it he said you'd never marry anyone but him. He threatened to do all manner of things, Jane. I was so frightened. He was like a wild man. I daren't tell his father! But I had to come and talk to you about it.'

'I'm glad you decided to, Mrs Denny.' Jane was cold inside. She took a deep breath in an attempt to compose herself. 'I expect you'll find Steve was just talking! No doubt the news hurt him, but it will wear off.'

'That's what I thought at the time, but after he'd had a sleep he prowled around the house like an animal, muttering threats. I really believe his mind is breaking up under the strain of loving you and all the drinking he's been doing.'

'But what can we do?' Jane demanded. 'I want to see Steve back to normal as much as you. Have you any suggestions how we can help him?'

'Help him?' the woman echoed. 'I think it's too late for that. I'll settle for stopping him doing something drastic that will ruin your life as well as his.'

The silence that followed the sharp words filled Jane with fear. She pictured Steve's face, and couldn't bring herself to condemn him. She was responsible for his condition, even though no blame could be attached to her. But something would have to be done before he talked or thought himself into a mental position from which he could not retreat, from which drastic action would prove to be his only outlet.

'I think I'll have a word with my uncle, Mrs Denny,' she said at length. 'If he could come and talk to Steve it might help. But failing that, I don't see what remedy would be effective.'

'You obviously don't see this as seriously as I do,' came the swift reply. 'My intention is to see the police and tell them about it before something happens. I know Steve, and it's the only way to stop him.'

Jane stared at the woman in speechless fear. So it was worse than she imagined. She set her teeth into her bottom lip as she watched worry chasing itself across Mrs Denny's face. Then she nodded slowly.

'Mrs Denny, do you know Jim Fraser?' she asked.

'Yes. He used to go to school with the rest of you. Why? Can he help?'

'He's a policeman now. I saw him on his beat the other day. But he is a friend, and perhaps I can get him to talk to Steve unofficially. If we made an official enquiry there could be trouble, and a lot of unwanted publicity. It might also have the wrong effect on Steve. If you'll leave the matter with me, I'll see what I can do about it, and I'll come and see you again. It will save you waiting around here.'

'I'd rather come here,' came the worried reply. 'I wouldn't want you to run the risk of meeting Steve at my home.'

'All right. You're on the phone. I'll call you when I have something to tell you. Will that be all right?'

'It might work. Steve needs something to bring him back to his senses. A talk by a policeman might do just that. But don't waste any time, Jane, I implore you. I didn't like the way Steve acted today, and that's a fact. So long as you understand that it is serious, then it's all right.'

'I'll get on to it right away,' Jane said, and sat back in her seat as Mrs Denny arose. 'Don't worry so much. Perhaps Steve didn't mean it.'

'I know better than that, or I wouldn't have worried you with it,' came the reply, and the woman departed, leaving Jane with a mind filled with intangible fears.

Was this the unforeseen circumstance

that she had been afraid of? It came to Jane that she had been worried all along that something would arise to spoil her future. Now she had dark thoughts that seemed to tell her that the dream of love might be coming to an end!

9

Constable Fraser was tall and power-fully built, and he seemed to fill Jane's office as he entered after her last patient had gone. A telephone call to the station had elicited his home number, and a call there brought him quickly from his fireside and family. He stared at her with a grin on his handsome face, and Jane held out a hand to him as he advanced upon her.

'Hello, Jim! It's so nice to see you again. It must be years since we last met!'

'I heard you were back, but I haven't had the chance to see you,' he replied. 'You're getting married next year, so I've heard. Let me congratulate you before we go any further. I know Doctor Carson slightly, at least he's treated me once or twice, and I think he's a very nice person. I hope you'll both be happy.' He paused. 'But you've got something worrying you, Jane. What's wrong?'

'I'm sorry to call you out when you're off duty,' she began, but he waved a quick hand.

'Don't let that worry you. I'm a policeman twenty-four hours a day.'

'I didn't want to make an official enquiry,' she began.

'All right. It won't go any further than this room, unless you want it to. Now what's the trouble?'

Jane explained about Steve Denny, omitting nothing. Jim Fraser nodded slowly as she lapsed into silence afterwards.

'I've been keeping an eye on Steve,' he said. 'Of course, we're all friends, and I don't want to see any of our old crowd getting into trouble. I've had reports from other people that he's drinking far too much and making a general nuisance of himself, but I didn't know the cause of it. You know as well as I that he's always been a very steady man. This is a great pity, but of course he's got to be stopped. Don't blame yourself in any way, Jane. You can't hold yourself responsible for what he does. I'll go along this evening and have a word with him. You'd be surprised just what effect that sort of thing has. A gentle reminder often shakes them back to their proper senses, and I expect that's all Steve needs.'

'His poor mother is worrying herself sick,' Jane said. 'We'll all be very grateful if you could do something, Jim.'

'I'll let you know how I get on,' he said. 'I won't mention your name because that might do more harm than good. I'll put it to him generally that his behaviour isn't all that it should be. I can approach him as a friend.'

'Thank you. It is a bit worrying to learn of something like this, especially when the man concerned is an old friend. It's a pity he didn't find himself a girl before I came home.'

'He never was one for the girls,' Jim

Fraser said. 'I seem to remember as long ago as the time you were seeing Roger Keeble that Steve used to say he wished he was in Roger's shoes as far as you were concerned. It's a pity he didn't approach you in those days. It would have cleared the air a bit. I suppose he's been brooding about all of this, and it hasn't done him any good. Do you think he needs medical treatment?'

'I haven't seen him for some time, but the last time I saw him the signs were becoming obvious that he had to ease up or pay the penalty.'

'Well, I'll be getting along, and I'll call on him right now. I'll give you a ring or drop by when you're around, Jane. Goodbye now, and the best of luck for next year.'

'Thanks, Jim.' Jane saw him out, and she felt much easier as she prepared to leave. There were no more patients, and she had arranged to call at Philip's house when she was finished.

Leaving Milly to lock up, Jane got

into her car and drove through the town. She felt tired, and worry had added its weight to her. When she reached Philip's, she locked the car and went to the door. After knocking, she tried the door, but it was locked, and she frowned. Surely Philip hadn't forgotten that she was meeting him here! She rang again, and waited several minutes before she felt certain he was not at home. Then she turned away and went to sit in her car. Perhaps he had been called out!

Thirty minutes later her patience ran out and she started the car and drove away. Going back to the surgeries, she discovered the building locked. She found her keys and entered, going into the receptionist's office to use the telephone. She called the farm and spoke to her mother, enquiring if Philip had arrived there, and Mrs Ashford replied that she hadn't seen him. Jane rang John's home. He was on call, and answered the phone immediately.

'Philip?' he said. 'No, I haven't seen

him or heard from him this evening. Have you lost him?'

'We arranged that I would go around to his house when I finished the evening surgery,' Jane replied.

'And he didn't ring you before you were through! That's odd. Where could he have gone?'

'That's what I'm wondering,' Jane said. 'It isn't like him to go off somewhere without letting me know about it. He wouldn't have gone to see a patient, would he?'

'Not while I'm on call,' came the smooth reply. 'But why are you so worried, Jane? Surely you can let the man out of your sight for an evening here and there!'

'It isn't that, John,' she replied. 'But we made firm arrangements about this evening, and if he'd had to go somewhere he would have telephoned first to say so.'

'Well, I'm sorry I can't help you at the moment,' John replied. 'Where are you now?'

'Back at the surgery.'

'Are you going on home afterwards?'

'Yes. I'll check his house again, then go on home. If you happen to hear from him tell him where I'll be, will you, please?'

'Certainly. But don't worry. Sometimes a man needs to go off alone.'

'Thank you, John. Good night!' Jane hung up. She glanced around the office, and was about to leave when she heard the outer door open. Relief swept through her. It would be Philip! She left the office and peered towards the door. Despite the early evening and the last of the twilight, it was quite gloomy inside the building. She could make out a figure standing on the doormat, his back to the closed door, and she felt a lump come into her throat. 'Philip?' she demanded.

'Him! It's always Philip these days,' came the thick reply.

Jane froze as she recognised Steve's voice. She moistened her lips quickly, moving back to the office doorway.

'Steve! Are you all right?' she demanded. 'Do you want to see me?'

'That's why I'm here.' He did not move, and his very attitude put fear into Jane.

'Well, I'm in rather a hurry,' she replied. 'I've just had a call to visit a patient. It's an emergency.'

'Then they'll have to get one of the others! I want to talk to you, Jane.'

'It'll have to wait, I'm afraid. Why don't you come and see me in the morning? Or I'll call at your house, if you like.'

'It's too late for that!' He came forward then, out of the shadows, and Jane stood firm although her every inclination was to keep out of his reach. There was something in the atmosphere that warned her to be careful. Steve had reached a crisis. 'I've loved you for years, Jane, and I can't stand by and watch you marry a complete stranger. First it was Roger Keeble, but he dropped out of it. You were away for years, and all that time I loved you. I tried to go away myself, to forget you, but it didn't work, and I'm slowly putting myself into my grave because I can't forget you.'

'Then you do need help, Steve,' she replied, keeping her tones even, her fears out of her voice. 'Let me make an appointment for you with someone who can help you.'

'A psychiatrist?' he scoffed. 'Is that what I've come down to?' He laughed bitterly. 'I'm living in hell, Jane! Nothing else matters now. If I can't have you, I'm going to see that no one else will.'

'Have you been drinking again?' she demanded.

'Again?' he echoed, and laughed. 'I never stop these days. Have you no pity, Jane? Don't you care about me in the least?'

'I do care more than you realise,' she replied. 'It's not easy to stand by and watch an old friend sink down. I want to help you.'

'There's only one way you can help

me,' he retorted thinly. 'Marry me! Stop running around with Carson and come to me.'

'That's out of the question, I'm afraid,' Jane said firmly. 'It's something you've just got to face up to, Steve. Everyone is pulling for you. Think of your mother! She's worried half out of her mind about you. You've got so much to look forward to.'

'I've got nothing. You're all I want!' He spoke simply, and Jane felt pity for him rise inside her. But she had a premonition of danger, and realised that she had better humour him.

'Let me drive you home, Steve,' she said. 'I promise we'll talk about this again later. I do have a patient to see. It is an emergency. Please don't keep me now, I beg you!'

'You're not going anywhere.' He turned swiftly and locked the door at his back. Jane took a deep breath and stepped back into the office, slamming the stout door and locking it. There was a Yale lock on the door, and she was relieved as it clicked solidly. She heard Steve come to the door and try it, and then he spoke through the panels in a low, determined voice, the tones of which scared Jane more than if he had shouted or raved at her. 'Open this door or I'll kick it in,' he said.

There was an iron grille at the wicket-type window in the wall through which the receptionist spoke to the patients when they came. Jane went to it and peered through, catching a glimpse of Steve as he shook the door to test its strength.

'Steve, I'll put through a nine-nine-nine call to the police if you don't get out of here. If you don't care about yourself, then think of your parents. Any publicity through this would put an end to a lot of things.'

'Open the door,' he snapped, coming to the grille and shaking it with powerful hands. 'I've been thinking about this for a long time, Jane, and it's the only way. I can't live without you. I feel sick through and through. This has been driving me crazy for weeks now.'

Jane picked up the telephone receiver and began to dial the emergency number. She watched him intently, saw that his face was impassive and set, and knew that he was not in complete control of his actions. She didn't want to call the police, but she dared not let this get out of hand.

'Are you leaving?' she demanded. 'In a moment I shall be talking to the police.'

She could hear the operator's voice demanding which service was required, and the metallic tones sounded across the office. Steve stared at her, gripping the grille with powerful fingers, and his lips twisted as he considered. He was stiff with determination, and Jane could imagine the thoughts and impulses running through his mind. Then he relaxed and his shoulders sagged.

'I'm going,' he said. 'I'm sorry, Jane, but I meant you no harm. I was only trying to scare you.'

'I'm sorry, I dialled the wrong

number,' Jane said to the operator, and hung up. She did not move from the table, and kept her hand upon the telephone. 'I want you to leave now, Steve,' she said. 'If you do so without further trouble, then I shan't breathe a word to anyone. But if you ever come near me again I'll report the matter to the police. Do you understand?'

'All right!' All the life seemed to have gone out of him. He was leaning against the grille like a puppet with broken strings. 'I'm going. I said I was sorry.' He turned slowly and went to the door, and Jane moved to the grille in order to watch him. She saw him open the door, and advised him to leave the lock so the door would be locked automatically when he closed it. He stared at her for a moment, then shrugged. 'Goodbye,' he said dismally.

Jane did not relax. He slammed the door and she heard the lock click. Then his receding footsteps sounded, and she heaved a sigh of relief and relaxed weakly, dropping into a chair and clasping her hands together to stop their trembling. She felt sick and cold inside, and thought the reaction was going to claim her senses. There was a roaring sound in her ears and a darkness closed in about her. But she fought it off, and slowly her senses returned to normal. A few moments later she felt strong enough to stand up. But she dared not leave the office. She switched on a light and stood in the centre of the room, trying to recollect her scattered wits.

Had he really intended only scaring her? Jane recalled the dreadful moments when he had confronted her. She didn't think that had been his intention. If she hadn't darted into the office and locked the door she might possibly be lying dead at this very moment. The knowledge shocked her deeply. It was incredible that the incident had happened. But she knew now that Mrs Denny's fears were not unfounded. She really knew her son!

But what was to be done about it?

Jane knew she could not just ignore it. Jim Fraser! He would have to be told. Perhaps he could put some sense into Steve. Jane felt her optimism return, and the shock in her began to recede. She was about to unlock the office when she heard a hand trying the door outside. She froze against the door, holding her breath. But the outer door was locked, and that relieved her.

A hand knocked at the door, and she wondered if Steve had returned. She left the office and approached the outer door warily, half-expecting it to be kicked open without warning. Moistening her lips, she took a deep breath. When she called, her voice was thick with tension and almost unrecognisable.

'Who is there?' she demanded.

'It's Philip!'

Relief took the strength out of her legs, and Jane gulped and tried to compose herself as she opened the door. Philip stepped inside, his face grim in the reflected light coming from the office. He stared at her, his brow furrowed, and Jane wondered if her face was giving her away.

'What's going on, Jane?' he demanded.

'Going on?' she echoed.

'What do you mean, Philip?'

'You're here late. Why have you locked yourself in?'

'I came back here after I found you were not at home,' she replied, frowning. 'I rang the farm, and then called Uncle John to find out if they'd seen anything of you. We did make arrangements for me to come round to you when I finished evening surgery, remember, Philip?'

'I remember quite well,' he retorted. 'I was waiting for you when I had a telephone call. A Mr Sennitt said he was calling on your behalf. You were attending his wife in the village of Swanstoft and you wanted me to go there. He promised to be by the phone box in the village to show me the way to his house. When I got out there I could see no one, and when I made enquiries in the local pub I was assured no one by the name of Sennitt lived in the village.'

Jane was speechless as she stared at him. He was very angry, and it was understandable. It was bad enough for a doctor to be called out in an emergency, but to find such a call was a false alarm was infuriating.

'I know nothing of it,' she replied. 'I went around to your house when I finished here.'

'What's that smell?' he demanded. He was sniffing curiously. 'Spirits,' he mused. 'Have you had the town drunk in here, or are you a secret drinker?'

Jane saw he was not joking, and she did not reply. He looked around, and she clearly saw the suspicion in his pale eyes.

'There's been no one here since I returned,' she said.

'Do you mind if I look around?' he demanded. 'Perhaps someone has got in unknown to you.'

'But the door was locked,' she

pointed out. She expelled her breath quickly. 'But go ahead. Strange things do happen. It would be better if you looked around, just in case. I'll wait here for you.'

He stared at her for a moment, and such was the expression on his face that Jane was hard put to recognise him. He looked like a stranger as he moved away from her. She remained where she was, and he searched the ground floor, looking everywhere a man might conceal himself. Then he went up the stairs, and she listened to the sound of his feet overhead. When he came back to her he seemed a little easier. He even smiled thinly, but he still looked quite upset.

'I'm sorry I lost my temper,' he said stiffly. 'It was no joke travelling ten miles, wondering what the devil could have happened to have you asking for my help. Then I waited around a long time before making enquiries.'

'And then you come back to find me locked in and the place smelling like the inside of a brewery,' she ended.

He smiled again, and shook his head. 'I'd like to know the object of that false alarm,' he said. Then he stiffened. 'I wonder if it was done to get me out of the way while someone burgled my house?'

'Let's go and see!' Jane was touched by the same urgency, although she had an idea in the back of her mind that Steve Denny might be responsible for that call.

'My car is outside,' he said. 'We'll pick up yours later. Come on.'

Jane went with him and they drove to his house. As she had expected, there was nothing amiss, and Philip was relieved as they stood together in the sitting-room. A low fire burned in the grate, for the evening was cool.

'I'm sorry, Jane, for behaving as I did at the surgery,' he said. 'But it was an infuriating experience. The trouble is, one starts wondering if every call is of a similar nature. Someone has a twisted sense of humour all right, and I'd twist his neck if I ever found out who it was.'

Jane knew in her heart that it must have been Steve ensuring that he wouldn't be disturbed when he came to see her, and as yet she hadn't found the time to consider what might have happened if she hadn't locked herself in the office. It was obvious, without thought, that she couldn't permit herself to be found in a similar situation by Steve. Something had to be done about him before he overstepped the mark. A tragedy might have occurred this evening! She felt her pulses race as she relived some of the fear that had caught up with her.

Philip wasn't prepared to forget his experience either, and they sat down to discuss their future plans, with Philip harping back to the false alarm at every odd moment. Jane found her nerves were taut, almost too tense, and her hands trembled from time to time as she thought of Steve's visit to the surgery.

By the time she decided to go home

she had thought out what she must do. In the morning she would see Jim Fraser and find out what he had accomplished. If he had failed to see Steve, then she would acquaint him with the further incidents, and no doubt he would take a grave view of what had happened.

Philip drove her back to the surgery to collect her car, and Jane kissed him goodnight in his car before getting out of it to go to her own. She glanced fearfully around the shadowy yard, but nothing happened to raise her alarm, and she got into the car and drove thankfully out to the road. Philip flicked his headlights in farewell as she drove away, and Jane sighed deeply as she went home.

She was apprehensive on the lonely country road, for her mind was not easy. Steve had a car, and she wouldn't put it past him to wait for her somewhere between the town and the farm. But she would not stop for anything or anyone, she resolved, and sped along with her hands gripping the wheel. When she reached the farm she felt quite weak from anticipation. But nothing happened and she left the car in the yard and hurried into the house. She didn't relax until she was in bed, and then some of the tension still clung to her mind.

10

Next day it was her turn to do the rounds, and she went into the office early to get her list from Milly. She was determined to take the incidents of the previous night a step farther, which meant approaching Jim Fraser. Jane left the surgery to start her rounds, and saw Jim in the High Street. She stopped the car and went after him. He was talking to a traffic warden, but smiled and came towards her when he spotted her.

'Hello, Jane,' he greeted. 'I didn't manage to see Steve last evening, but I had a good long talk with his parents, and they are going to take a stronger line with him. I will see him when I'm able, so don't think the matter will be allowed to slide.'

'If you had stayed at my surgery last evening you would have seen him, Jim,' Jane said slowly.

'You mean he came there after I called?' His eyes narowed as he tried to guess what was on her mind, and Jane drew a long breath. She was suddenly reliving the tensions again. 'What happened?' he demanded.

Jane told him all about it, including the false alarm that took Philip out of town.

'I see,' he said seriously when she had finished. 'This is getting too much. Jane, my advice to you is go along to the station and have a word with the Inspector. I ought to make a report of this myself, you know. But you mustn't take any chances. Mrs Denny tells me that Steve has developed an almost uncontrollable temper. Only yesterday he almost struck her when she was talking to him about his poor ways.'

'It seems as if he is losing control of himself,' Jane said. 'I don't want to start anything official, you understand.'

'I understand perfectly, Jane. In your position you can't afford any kind of publicity, but this must be checked. I'll go after him this morning, if you wish, and read the riot act to him, but if I do I shall have to report it. Then it will be out of my hands and yours.'

'I don't know what to do,' Jane confessed. 'I don't want to make trouble for Steve. He has enough of that already. But talking won't help. On the other hand, I wouldn't want Philip to know what really happened last night. I didn't tell him at the time, and it may seem odd to him if it came out now.'

'You can't afford to spare anyone's feelings, Jane. I'm doing less than my duty by not urging you to see the Inspector. If anything happened after this and it was discovered that I knew about the events leading up to it I would be on the carpet.' He shook his head. 'I promised you last night that I wouldn't take it any farther, Jane, and I'll stand by my word. But I earnestly implore you to consider the circumstances very carefully. If you really believe Steve was going to harm you last night, then report the matter officially. You owe it to yourself, and to your parents and future husband.'

His words struck deeply through Jane, and she nodded. 'I'll see the Inspector,' she said. 'I don't have time at the moment, but I'll call in some time today. Will that be all right?'

'I'll make a report to him in the meantime, so he'll have all the facts. That will save your time, Jane. But don't go back on your decision, will you?'

'No.' She shook her head. 'I had a real scare last night, and I wouldn't want it to be repeated. I'm not going to take any chances, Jim.'

'Good girl!' He patted her arm. 'Now you'd better move on because you're parked on double yellow lines.' He smiled as her expression changed, and escorted her back to the car, helping her into it and slamming the door. He stepped back and saluted her as she drove away.

Jane considered her future actions as

she went through the list of calls she had to make. She hurried as best she could in order to make some time, and in the early afternoon she drove into Haylingford and parked outside the police station. It seemed that Jim had made his report, because as soon as she gave her name at the desk she was shown into Inspector Teasdale's office.

She knew the Inspector by sight, and he greeted her cordially, an oldish man with a quiet air of efficiency and ability about him. He brought forward a chair for her, and Jane was conscious of deep trembling inside her as she waited for him to speak.

'I have Constable Fraser's report,' he said, studying her with keen blue eyes. 'I must say that I don't like the tone of this at all, and you're very wise to come forward. I have been getting some reports about Steve Denny's decline. He's been involved in a couple of fights lately, and there was some damage to private property in which he was involved.'

'I don't want to bring any charges against him, or anything like that,' Jane said. 'I thought a few words from someone in uniform might shake some sense into him.'

'That's possible, and it will be all we can do at the moment. Constable Fraser has offered to see Denny, but I have the feeling that, being a former friend, his warning may not carry enough weight, so I propose to see Denny myself, as soon as possible, and warn him to stay away from you. If that fails, then the only course is to take him before the court. I can understand your reluctance to do that, and I agree the best way would be to handle it as I've suggested. But be very careful in future, Doctor. Don't take any risks.'

'I certainly won't,' Jane said strongly. 'I got quite a scare last night, I can tell you.'

'I'm having some enquiries made about that false call that was put through to Doctor Carson last night,' Inspector Teasdale said. 'But there I don't expect any joy. I understand you want to keep the incidents of last night from the doctor. That is your decision, of course, but I wouldn't have any secrets from him, if I were you. It might lead to a lot of misunderstanding.'

'I know you're right, Inspector,' Jane said slowly, 'but I can't help thinking that the knowledge might stir up some trouble. Doctor Carson might go after Steve Denny himself, and that would be the worst possible action.'

'I agree with you there, Doctor.' The Inspector got to his feet. 'Look, leave it with me for a day or two. I'll go round and see Denny and give it to him straight. Then I'll have someone watching him for a bit. If he takes the hint all well and good, but if he shows any signs of maintaining his present outlook, then more drastic action will have to be considered.'

'Thank you, Inspector.' Jane took her leave, feeling only a little happier. She didn't think Steve would forget as easily as all that, and she would have to take precautions in future to ensure that she was not alone at any time when it was likely he might try to get to her.

She continued her round, and finished just before tea. Time seemed to hang heavily upon her as she went home. Philip was taking evening surgery, and was coming out to the farm later. She had tried to forget what happened to him the previous evening. She was certain in her own mind that Steve had been responsible for that false call. It could happen again at any time, to Philip or herself, and the next time Steve might be waiting to do something drastic. She shivered at the thought as she drove into the farmyard. She was on call herself tonight, and if Steve knew that then he had knowledge of her weakness. She wouldn't want to be caught alone on a country road after dark, and she had to answer any call that was put through to her.

But nothing happened that night. Philip called after he had finished at the surgery, and they spent an enjoyable evening with Jane's parents. After Philip went back to town, Jane went to bed and slept soundly until morning, there being no emergencies to disturb her. She awoke next morning to find the sky grey and threatening, and she was filled with worry as she prepared to go into town and take morning surgery.

But the weather was not an omen. During the morning Inspector Teasdale telephoned to explain his actions, and he reported that he had spoken to Steve and warned him against seeing Jane again. Steve had voiced his regrets for the incident and said he was going away again. He wouldn't make any effort to see her.

'Thank you, Inspector!' Jane could not keep a tremor of relief out of her voice.

'We'll be checking his movements to make sure he keeps his word,' the Inspector said. 'And don't take any chances, Doctor, to be on the safe side.'

'I won't.' Jane hung up with a feeling of hopefulness seeping through her breast. Now she could realise just how much of a strain she had been under in the past few days. She went back to work with vigour, and felt as if she had come happily through a great crisis.

The days passed slowly as she waited to find out if the news she had received from Inspector Teasdale was true. She didn't see Steve around, and ensured that she was not alone at any time when he might come upon her. Then the Inspector rang again to say that Steve had left the town. Mrs Denny had given him the address where Steve would be staying in London, and a check would be made to find out if he planned to stay there. Jane hung up with the feeling that all her worries were over.

Time seemed to gain momentum then, and with each succeeding day Jane slowly regained her former happiness. Worry vanished as if it had never been! Weeks went by and autumn gave way to winter. Soon they were looking forward to Christmas, and there was a rise in the number of patients they had to see as the season brought its customary ills. But Jane was sublimely happy. Preparations for the wedding were being made, and each succeeding week found some other facet of their love being substantiated.

Jane forgot about Steve Denny, and Philip occupied most of her free time. Then there was an epidemic of influenza, and they found almost double the number of patients to be visited. Christmas passed in a flurry of making visits, and the festive season was past almost before Jane realised that it had come upon them. Philip stayed at the farm for a week, although they had little time in which to celebrate, and after Christmas had gone into the past Jane began to look forward to her important date in March.

Towards the end of January, Philip decided they ought to start looking for a home, and they spent some of their off-duty afternoons looking around the various properties and visiting estate agents. Advice was forthcoming from every quarter, but eventually they settled upon a bungalow in the village of Winchley, only two miles from her parents' farm.

After Philip had attended to the formalities, Jane busied herself during her free time with the great job of furnishing the place. It proved that Philip had little or no idea of colour schemes and the like, and Jane enlisted the aid of her mother. Together they worked out schemes for every room, and Philip employed Mr Denny to put the work in hand. With the decorating finished, they began to furnish, and Jane enjoyed the trips to town and the ordering and examining of stock. Slowly the bungalow was filled with furniture and furnishings, and it began to look like a home. With full central heating installed, they had the system working on odd days to keep the bungalow aired.

Jane spent every spare moment at the bungalow, and when there was nothing to do she went there to just look around, her thoughts filled with anticipation and her mind set upon the happy future.

February was a dreary month, but to Jane it seemed that the sun was always shining. She began to feel nervous as the days passed, to bring her particular date that much nearer, but she knew without doubt that she loved Philip and that he loved her. They were just right for one another. The entire winter had proved it to them, and there were no doubts in Jane's heart.

Then John Ashford was taken ill! Jane had just returned to the farm after finishing her round when the telephone rang, and John himself spoke faintly.

'Jane, can you come to me?' he demanded. His voice was almost unrecognisable. 'I'm at home. I feel very ill.'

The line went dead before she could speak, and for a moment Jane was frozen in shock. Then she hung up and called for her mother.

'I'd better come with you, Jane,' Mrs

Ashford said quickly. 'I'll just leave a message with Mrs Gartside for your father.'

They were silent as they drove to town, and Jane was filled with a strange foreboding. When they reached John's house Mrs Ashford hurried in while Jane parked the car and took up her bag. The house was silent, filled with a strange atmosphere, when Jane entered, and she paused at the foot of the stairs and listened for sound of her mother. Then Mrs Ashford appeared from John's bedroom at the top of the stairs.

'Mother! What's wrong?' Jane hurried up the stairs at sight of Mrs Ashford's stricken face.

'John is dead!'

Jane stared at her mother in disbelief, then hurried into the bedroom. John lay upon the bed, and looked as if he were asleep. His collar was undone, but he was still wearing his jacket. Jane felt for his pulse, and then a heartbeat, but there was nothing. He was dead.

'Jane! What happened to him?' Mrs

Ashford was standing in the doorway, swaying in shock.

'Heart attack, by the looks of it,' Jane said, turning to help her mother to a chair. 'He wouldn't have known anything about it. I'd better ring Father, and let Philip know.'

'But it was so sudden.' Mrs Ashford's face was deathly white. 'Did he ever complain of feeling ill?'

'No.' Jane shook her head as she gazed at the motionless figure on the bed. 'Poor John! He's been working too hard! This winter was a great strain upon him. I ought to have watched him more carefully.'

'Don't blame yourself, Jane! He didn't show any symptoms. He never had a day's illness in his whole life.'

Jane went to the telephone to pass on the shocking news. Her father took her call at the farm, and a shocked silence ensued after Jane had told him of his brother's death. Then Charles told her he would be coming immediately. She rang Philip, who was at the surgery, and within a few minutes he arrived, white faced and grim, his eyes showing the same shock that gripped them all.

'It was his heart,' Philip confirmed after examining John. 'How old was he?'

'Sixty-two this year, in June,' Mrs Ashford said slowly. 'He was four years older than my husband.'

'I'll make out the death certificate.' Philip took Jane by the arm. 'Go and make your mother a nice cup of tea.' He led them both from the room. 'I'll do what's necessary here.'

Jane nodded, her mind in a turmoil. Shock was a clogging safety valve applied by Nature to protect the mind from such blows, and she moved as if in a nightmare to do as she was bidden. When her father arrived Mrs Ashford broke down, and they had to comfort her.

'Take your mother home, Jane,' Charles Ashford said. His face was grey with shock.

Jane nodded. She felt that she wanted

to get away from this house. Death was no stranger to her, and especially during the past winter weeks when the death rate from influenza had been high among the more senior of their patients. But this particular death, shocking with the unexpectedness of it all, struck deeply into her heart. She took her mother home, and stayed there herself, filled with an uncharacteristic dread that held her powerless and afraid.

When her father arrived home in late evening they were all feeling slightly less shocked, but the atmosphere was one of incredulity. John was dead and gone from them! It was a short, simple thought, but it attacked the very roots of their understanding.

The ensuing days were far busier, with John's absence from the practice, and that was a blessing in some respects, for it helped Jane keep her mind from her uncle's death. She was almost run off her feet, and Philip talked of advertising for someone to take John's place. Jane was unable to bring herself to talk about the future, but after John's funeral the tension and the shock seemed to lessen.

Life went on regardless! That was a bitter lesson that Jane learned as the days passed. She missed John greatly. He had always been very kind and understanding, and had exerted a great influence upon her life. For years she and he had looked forward to the time when she would join him in his practice, but only a few months had passed since she qualified, and now he was gone and she was left to carry on alone. It seemed very unfair to Jane that he should come to an untimely end. He had been a man who sacrificed his life to the service of his fellows. He had been a good man, and his thoughts had always been turned outwards, away from himself. His passing left a great gap in Jane's life.

There was only one month to the day of her wedding! It was two weeks since John had been buried in the quiet little churchyard in Winchley. Now the shock had gone completely, leaving a dull ache in her heart, a void in her mind that nothing could fill. Time would take care of it, she knew, and Time was never in a hurry. But the necessity to go on living, to make plans for her own future, took her through the difficult days. Work was demanding, and she and Philip were kept busy for many hours each day.

Then a new doctor arrived in response to the adverts they had placed in the medical papers. She and Philip saw several candidates, and selected a middle-aged man who was moving from his own practice because his wife had died. Jane felt a sympathy for Doctor Jones, for she greatly missed John. She could understand this man's reason for wanting to uproot himself from all his memories. They agreed that Doctor Jones would join them in a month, and he went away much happier than when he had arrived.

'You know, Jane, that we're not going

to have a honeymoon,' Philip said one evening when they were at the bungalow. Jane was on call, and she had arranged for her mother to ring her here at the bungalow if she were needed. 'Doctor Jones won't be arriving until after the wedding. The locum will be here, but we can't go off and leave him to try and cope with everything. Would you like to postpone the wedding until we're settled in the practice, or shall we get married and carry on as if a honeymoon didn't matter?'

'All the arrangements are made,' Jane replied. 'Let's keep to our original date, Philip. We can always have a honeymoon later.'

'Right you are!' He smiled. 'You're the boss!'

'I won't have that,' she replied, smiling faintly. 'It's going to be a fifty-fifty relationship.'

'Poor Jane! You've been so busy these past weeks! But there's nothing I can do to alleviate the situation. I'm working flat out as it is. But I'm really glad that we formed this group practice. You'd have been in a mess if you'd been left alone in the practice.'

'You've been a great help,' Jane said softly. 'I don't know what I should have done without you, Philip. Fate surely smiled at me the day we met.'

'I'm not complaining at my lot,' he replied. 'You're the most wonderful girl in the world, Jane. Things are working out better than I could ever have hoped. I'm a very fortunate man.'

'We won't get a lot of time to be together until the practice has settled down again,' she mused. 'You won't mind, Philip?'

'Not in the least. We're both doctors, and dedicated to our work. So long as we're together, it's all that matters.'

Jane felt happier then than she had done for some time. Her grief at John's death was sinking a little into perspective. The approaching date of her wedding was beginning to loom, and March came in blustery and impatient to follow February into history.

There seemed so little time to attend to personal affairs that Jane lost contact with her friends. She saw Dorothy Beck occasionally because she made the time to have her hair done, and it was wonderful to relax under one of the dryers. Kay Lanham had taken orders for wedding dresses, and in the very near future they would be ready for the first fittings. Time seemed to gain momentum, and the great day would be upon them before they realised it.

Dropping in at the hairdresser's one afternoon, Jane settled down to spend a quiet hour in Dorothy's skilled hands, and they chatted about the wedding. It still seemed like a dream to Jane. She had the unreal feeling that the day itself would never dawn.

'Have you heard that Roger Keeble is getting engaged, Jane?' Dorothy demanded at length.

'No!' Jane stiffened in the chair.

'It's true! She's a farmer's daughter. We don't know her. She's a stranger.'

'I don't think any girl who knows Roger's past would marry him,' Jane said. 'But I wish him luck.'

'And the girl! She'll need it.' Dorothy shook her head. 'I didn't think Roger would ever take the plunge. It's strange, you know, how most of our crowd haven't married yet. But you've started a vogue, it seems. You're getting married in a couple of weeks, and Roger is considering it. I wonder if I'll ever get the chance?'

'I don't see why not!' Jane glanced up at her friend. 'Are you making efforts to meet someone?'

'Not really. I'm much too busy with the shop. You know how it is, and there doesn't seem to be any eligible men around this town. Perhaps I ought to move out, like Steve Denny did.'

'Have you heard anything of him since he went away again?' Jane asked casually.

'Yes.' Dorothy lowered her voice. 'I heard that he's gone into a nursing home for treatment. He couldn't leave drink alone. It was strange how he suddenly went off the rails. It coincided with the time you returned home, Jane. You don't think Steve was secretly in love with you, do you?'

'I hardly think that's likely. Steve and I were good friends. But he never gave any indication of loving me.' Jane swallowed the lump that came to her throat. She pictured Steve's face, and knew she was the cause of his troubles. He had always been a steady person, ready to help anyone who needed it.

'Well, he's in the best place. It's a weakness that has to be cured. I hope he'll get on all right.' Dorothy lowered her voice again. 'You know, Jane, there was a time when I could have fallen in love with Steve Denny. But he just wasn't interested. Now if he had found himself a good girl and settled down he wouldn't have landed up where he is.'

Jane did not reply, but she felt stifled. Guilt came easily to her, although she knew she could hardly be blamed for the way things had turned out for

Steve. She was thoughtful when she left Dorothy and went back to the surgery to prepare for duty. Later she was going to the bungalow to light the furnace. With such damp weather the building had to be kept heated.

It all seemed grossly unfair to her, the way some lives were wasted and others carried extra burdens. But she could not complain for herself. She was happy with her lot. She loved her work and she was going to marry the man of her dreams. What more could she ask for? But even her happiness gave her a feeling of guilt. She had never known such joy before, and she was afraid that something would come to mar it.

When Inspector Teasdale called a week before the wedding to say that Steve Denny had disappeared from the nursing home where he had been receiving treatment, Jane thought her worst fears were about to come true. This was what she had secretly feared all the time!

11

Jane didn't say anything to Philip of her fears. For some obscure reason she wanted to keep that from him. They were both working under a great strain, and with the wedding approaching time seemed at a premium. But she was really worried as she drove around the villages to visit the patients. Everywhere she looked she thought she saw Steve Denny, but the days went by and there were no further reports of him. He had disappeared from the nursing home and hadn't been seen or heard of since.

Jim Fraser spoke to her when she stopped at some crossroads where he stood, and the subject was Steve Denny. He confirmed that Steve couldn't be traced, and there was a missing persons call out on him. He warned her to be careful and to call the station at the first hint of trouble.

'But I don't think he's come back this way,' he said reassuringly. 'Someone would have seen him, if he had. I expect he's lying low in London for some reason or other.'

'He could drink himself to death in a very short time,' Jane said slowly. 'I do hope they find him, and that they can cure him.'

'They can cure him only if he wants to be cured,' Jim Fraser said. 'How are you making out? You're being run off your feet, aren't you?'

'We are busy. But our new partner joins us next week.'

'And your wedding is Saturday! It'll be a working honeymoon, won't it?'

'I'm afraid it will be!' Jane nodded.

'Well, all the best. I hope you'll be very happy, Jane.'

'Thank you, Jim. But I shall be glad when it's all over.'

'That's how we all feel when the great day approaches,' he said with a laugh. 'I've seen your bungalow in the village. It's a lovely place. You've done it up really well inside.'

'Are you watching it?' Jane demanded.

'Not personally, but I do know the Inspector has asked the village policeman to keep an eye on things in your area. That's since Steve got out of the nursing home. If he does come snooping around, we'll get him.'

Jane suppressed a shiver. 'Do you think I ought to worry Philip with it?' she demanded.

'You haven't told him?' Jim looked surprised.

'I decided to keep it away from him ever since Steve caught me alone in the surgery. After that I just couldn't broach it without making it appear worse than it really was.'

'There's something in that. Well, let's hope there'll be no need to tell him anything. Did the Inspector ask you to notify the local constable if you were called out at night?'

'He did mention it, but I haven't done so. I don't want to be a bother to anyone. Nothing has happened so far.

But I do keep my fingers crossed.'

Jane went on, her thoughts filled with Steve Denny. She felt so sorry for him! In the back of her mind was the thought that he wouldn't do her any harm! But the fears of that encounter with him warned her that she would be foolish to take chances. She would never forget those tense moments, when it had been touch and go, in the gloomy office. At lunch she saw Philip, and they talked together about the end of the week. It was Tuesday, and they were to be married on Saturday.

'We'd better keep the central heating going all this week, Jane,' Philip said. 'Moving in on Saturday, we'll want the place to be aired.'

'I expect one of us will be called out on an emergency,' she said with a smile.

'But we'll be able to take it easy when Doctor Jones joins us. He and the locum will be able to handle things while we snatch a couple of days away.'

'The locum is arriving on Friday, isn't he?' Jane watched his face, wondering exactly how Philip felt about everything now the time was arriving. For herself, she was happy and filled with anticipation.

'That's right. From what I saw of him when he came down, I'd say he'll make a good job of everything. We'll be able to go away with easy minds.'

'We really could do with four doctors in the practice, don't you think?' Jane queried.

'Now that two of us will be married, yes,' Philip said with a smile. 'But remember that before you came back to the town your uncle and I were the only doctors.'

'Poor Uncle John!' Jane slipped into Philip's arms. 'I wish he could have seen the wedding.'

'I grew very fond of him in the short time that I knew him, Jane. I shall always appreciate the way you came into my life on that Sunday. I was miserable and ready to call it off. I'd never felt more miserable in my life. Then I happened to look from the window, and I saw your car parked outside. Your face was like an angel's, I can tell you.'

'Tell me more, Philip,' she whispered. 'I was attracted to you, and that's why I was outside your house that day. Something seemed to compel me to come.'

'It was Fate,' he said, kissing her gently. 'The months have flown by, really, and everything has been working out as if a greater hand than yours or mine controlled the events.' He smiled as he searched her face. 'I love you, Jane. I would never have believed it possible that a woman could make such an impact upon a man. I never believed in love until I met you. Now I'm a convert.'

'I should hope so!' She clung to him, pressing her face against his shoulder and closing her eyes. 'You're marrying me at the end of the week. I should hope you do believe in love.'

'It is a real love match,' he said gently, stroking her dark hair. 'I often try to picture myself in later years, without you, and it's dreadful. I wish we weren't working so hard these days. You're looking quite strained, you know. Are you sure you haven't any secret worries? I know you've had a lot to face, what with John's death and all!'

'I'm all right,' she said. 'It is a bit of a strain, and having the wedding to think about. That's nerve racking, you know! I suppose it won't mean a thing to you!'

'Don't you believe it, dearest!' His eyes twinkled. 'I'm getting weak at the knees already.'

'And I believe you.' Jane tilted her face for a kiss, and then she sighed. 'I'd better be on my way now. I've got a lot to do as it is.'

'I'm going around to my house when I've finished evening surgery,' he told her. 'There's still a lot of stuff I want to go through, although there's no hurry. It doesn't matter if I haven't finished before the end of the week. We can always get it ready for sale later. But I do want to have all the odds and ends cleared up.'

'Tidy habits make for a tidy mind,' she said, disengaging herself from his embrace. 'I'll come there after tea. About seven-thirty?'

'I ought to be there by then,' he agreed. 'But ring me first at the surgery, about six-thirty. I'll have a better idea of what's facing me at that time.'

'I'll drop into the bungalow on my way in,' Jane said. 'If I attend to the furnace early, it will go through until some time tomorrow.'

'You're getting quite expert on that side of running a house,' he observed. 'It'll be a comfort to know I have a wife who doesn't really need a man around for the chores.'

'I think you'll turn up trumps, Philip,' she replied in similar vein. 'You'll be thoroughly domesticated. I can see you now, getting the washing in and doing the ironing.'

'Do you think we'll have any time for that sort of thing?' he demanded.

Jane was smiling to herself as she went out to finish her round. She had no qualms about the future. She and Philip were ideally suited. That much she had learned during the past months. Her heart felt light and gay as she drove through the sunny afternoon. Spring was in the air. Winter had relaxed its grip, and that period when it seemed neither one thing nor the other was beginning to pass. She took a deep breath and let her thoughts drift over the very near future. On Saturday afternoon she would be going into the church! All she hoped was that no one in the town would need a doctor urgently at that time. It would be dreadful if she or Philip had to run from the church to grab a medical bag and chase off to attend a patient. She smiled at the thought, although it would not be funny if it came to pass.

The afternoon seemed unreal to her. In fact, the overshadowing weekend made everything seem dreamlike. It was like awaiting the dawn of long-awaited holidays — the first time abroad or some wonderful treat that had been long in coming! Jane's heart had been beating faster than normal for days now, and she hoped the feeling would last long into married life.

By tea-time she was through, and she made her way back to the farm. When she reached home she parked the car, but left her medical bag in it. Her mother appeared on the step as Jane approached.

'Telephone, Jane,' Mrs Ashford called. 'I saw you coming.' She smiled apologetically. 'The caller is holding on.'

Jane cast her mind back over the day. She hadn't forgotten anyone, so this had to be an emergency. She went into the house and took up the receiver.

'This is Doctor Ashford,' she said.

'Jane, I've got to see you.' It was a man's voice, and Jane froze as she recognized Steve Denny's voice. She glanced around, but her mother had gone back into the sitting-room.

'Steve! Where are you?' she demanded.

'That doesn't matter. But I've got to see you,' came the terse reply. 'I know you're getting married on Saturday.'

'It wouldn't help either of us to meet again,' she said, and a tremor ran through her. 'Why have you left that nursing home, Steve? Don't you want to get well?'

'So you believe it's an illness, do you?' He chuckled softly, and the sound was frightening in her ear.

'Steve, you won't try anything foolish, will you?' she demanded. 'The police are watching me all the time, and have been since you disappeared from the nursing home. Don't do anything that will cause trouble for you. Think of your parents. Your mother must be worried out of her wits by now.'

'I want to see you, Jane.'

'I'm sorry, but that's out of the question.' She bated her breath, and could hear the blood pounding in her temples. 'Steve, try to do the right thing. No one wants to see you get better more than I do.'

'It's your fault I'm in this state,' he retorted almost angrily. 'If you had agreed to marry me instead of that stranger I would be all right today. I'd have my business and be in good health. But now I'm nothing!'

There was no answer to that outbreak, and Jane was tempted to hang up on him, but she was afraid he might go off at a tangent and do something desperate. She made a last attempt to get through to him.

'Where are you, Steve? Why do you want to see me?'

'Why do you think?' He laughed, and the sound of it sent a chill along her spine. 'I said a long time ago that if I couldn't have you, then Carson wouldn't. You're not marrying him on Saturday, Jane. I promise you that. And let me tell you something else. If you tell the police about me, then something drastic will happen.'

'I shall inform the police,' she said

angrily. 'You're insane, Steve, to talk like this!'

There was a click and the line went dead. Jane listened to the burring sound, her senses reeling. The nightmare was about to engulf her! She set her teeth into her bottom lip as she wondered what to do. Then she dialled the local police station and a moment later she was talking to Inspector Teasdale. After telling him about Steve's call, Jane asked what she ought to do.

'It's a pity you didn't arrange to meet him somewhere, then call me,' the Inspector said. 'Now you've put his back up, and there's no telling what he'll do. But that's nothing to worry about. I'll send a man out to keep an eye on things. What will be your movements tonight, Doctor?'

'I'm on call,' she replied. 'I planned to go to my bungalow, then drive into Haylingford to Doctor Carson's home. I'll leave an account of my movements with my mother, who'll ring me if an emergency arises.'

'I see. Well, I'll want you to do better than that. Ring this office before you leave to go anywhere, and telephone after you've arrived. The messages will be relayed to the man watching you. And if Denny does get in touch with you again, then make arrangements to meet him, and let me know. I'll have men in the area so he can be picked up.'

'I'll do that,' Jane said, and rang off. She felt very nervous as she joined her mother in the sitting-room, but her composure was intact as she chatted about her day.

They had tea together, and afterwards Jane began to think of leaving. She wanted to go to the bungalow before dark. But when she was ready to leave, her mind objected and her nerve almost failed her. She could not help remembering the last time she had seen Steve Denny. He had intended her harm. Of that there was no doubt. She called Philip at the surgery, and learned that he would be finished by about seven. She arranged to see him at his house, and steeled herself as she rang the police station to report that she would be going now to the bungalow. She was asked how long she intended to remain at the bungalow, and she thought that was odd.

'Only about ten minutes,' she said. 'I have to light the furnace for the central heating. It usually takes about ten minutes by the time everything is done. Then I'm going to Doctor Carson's house in Haylingford.'

'Very well,' the anonymous voice at the other end replied. 'Thank you for calling, Doctor.'

Jane hung up and took her leave. She drove to the bungalow, and sat for a moment in the car, staring around, wondering if it would be safe for her to enter. Then she pulled herself together and flayed herself angrily. She would be a bundle of nerves if she didn't have courage. It was still daylight, although night was beginning to creep into the sky, and she walked resolutely up the short path and unlocked the front door. Once inside, she locked the door, and felt more secure as she went through to the kitchen, where the furnace was situated. She busied herself, losing her fear as she worked.

Once she paused, hearing a slight sound that might have been caused by a furtive step in one of the bedrooms. She froze, and in the ensuing silence she could hear her heart beating. Was someone in the bungalow with her? She hurriedly finished what she was doing and started to the front door. She tiptoed and her feet made no sound on the carpet in the narrow hall. The interior of the bungalow was gloomy, and panic filled her, stealing her last resource of nerve. Jane grabbed at the door to jerk it open, but it wouldn't budge, and she remembered that she had locked it. Her fingers trembled uncontrollably as she fumbled with the lock. There were icy shivers running up and down her spine, and her legs felt as if they had turned to water.

The door swung open and Jane gasped in relief as she went outside, pausing only to bang the door, but as she turned her back a figure appeared at her side from the bushes, and she caught her breath in shock. She was startled, but thought this was the policeman sent to watch out for her.

'Jane, I thought I'd catch you here.'

She went to pieces as she looked into Steve Denny's shadowed features. Her mouth opened as if she was going to scream, but no sound issued. She clasped her hands together, and gulped as she tried to speak normally.

'Steve, you startled me,' she said lamely.

'Let's go inside,' he said roughly. 'I said I've got to talk to you.' He paused and peered intently at her face. 'I'm not going to hurt you. What do you think I am? I'm in love with you.'

'I'm in a hurry, Steve,' she said. 'Couldn't you see that I came out in a hurry?'

'This won't take a minute,' he

retorted, and came forward to take her arm.

Jane turned instantly, as if to obey his wishes, but she darted forward into the bungalow and turned to slam the door in his face. He was ready for the move, and his foot came into the doorway just in time to prevent it closing. Like a startled deer, Jane fled into the kitchen. She ran to the back door and tried to turn the key. Steve's feet thundered in the hall, and he came bursting after her. With a little cry of fear, Jane realised that she couldn't get the door open, and she turned to face him, cowering against the door. He came towards her with a cry of pleasure on his lips.

'I told you there was no need to be afraid of me,' he said. 'I realise that whatever I do, you won't turn to me, so I'm not going to do anything but wish you luck in your marriage.'

She stared at him fearfully, not believing him. If he had wanted to congratulate her on her forthcoming marriage, then he would have called at the farm to do so. But she realised with an effort that she had to humour him at all costs.

'All right,' she said. 'But let's go out to my car. I am in an awful hurry, Steve.'

'You don't believe me,' he said thinly. 'You're afraid of me.'

'You scared me the last time we met,' she defended.

'I'm sorry about that. But you can forget it. Look, all I want to do is have a few words with you, and wish you luck. Have you got a couple of glasses? I've got a bottle of whisky here. We could drink to your happiness. I'd like that. I'm going back to the nursing home in the morning.'

'I don't like whisky,' Jane said. 'The very smell of it makes me ill. But I have some sherry in the lounge. Will you have some of that?'

'No. It's got to be whisky.' He produced a half-bottle from his pocket. 'Where are the glasses?'

'In the sideboard in the lounge.'

'Let's go through there.' He stepped aside for her to pass, and Jane steeled herself to go close to him. But he made no attempt to touch her, and she trembled as she crossed the hall to the lounge. He followed very closely, and she could hear his harsh breathing.

As Jane opened the lounge door the doorbell rang, the chimes jangling against her nerves. She stopped dead in surprise, and Steve grabbed her by the shoulder, his fingers digging into her soft flesh.

'Who the devil is that?' he demanded.

'I don't know, but probably my future husband,' she replied.

'Did you know he was coming?'

'No. He's on duty at the surgery in town, or should be.' Jane was beginning to feel hopeful. Perhaps it was the policeman the Inspector said would be watching out for her. 'Look, if you don't want to see anyone you can sneak out by the back door. You can always see me again.'

The doorbell rang again, and he

tightened his grip upon her shoulder. Jane set her teeth into her bottom lip. It was all she could do to prevent herself crying out in fear. But she knew she could not risk arousing him.

'I'm not leaving,' he hissed. 'Have some sense! I came here to kill you, and I'm going to do so. Don't you dare make a sound or I'll strangle you. This whisky I've got is poisoned. We're both going to die. I've got nothing to live for. You've driven me to distraction, Jane, and I want to die now. But I'm not going alone. Get those glasses, and be quiet about it. If you make a sound I'll kill you the hard way.'

His voice echoed in the hall, and Jane drew a shuddering breath. She moved slowly, his hand still upon her shoulder, and the gloom inside the house was now almost complete. The doorbell rang again, and he half-turned to glance along the hall. Jane sensed that his attention was momentarily gone from her, and she sprang forward into the lounge and turned to slam the door.

But he was quick despite his preoccupation with the unknown caller. Jane managed to get the door almost closed, but she jammed her foot against the bottom of the door as he came barging against it.

She threw her weight against the door, filled with desperation, and her breath was sobbing in her throat. She could hear Steve cursing under his breath, and he kept thrusting his weight against the door. Jane felt her foot slipping on the carpet, and knew despair, and then a hand touched her shoulder and she almost died of fright.

'I'm a policeman,' a soft voice whispered in her ear. 'Get back out of the way.'

A strong hand was placed against the door to hold it against Steve's efforts to force it open. Jane hurriedly got out of the way, tottering to the sofa and dropping upon it in the last stages of nervous exhaustion. She clenched her hands as she listened. The door was opened and Steve came blundering into the room. The policeman grappled with him, and Jane heard the man give his identification. Steve started yelling insanely, and the sounds of a terrific struggle ensued. The doorbell was ringing continuously now, and Jane forced herself into action.

Getting to her feet she switched on the table lamp on the sideboard, and turned to see Steve struggling with the unknown policeman. They were evenly matched, and Jane watched for a moment. Then she edged forward and awaited her chance to dash into the hall. She got past them and hurried to the front door, fumbling with the catch to unlock it. The next instant the door was open and Jim Fraser and another man were coming into the bungalow. They joined the fray and Steve was quickly overpowered and handcuffed. He was taken out.

Jane stood shivering in the hall, almost beside herself in fear. She was badly shocked, and Jim Fraser came to her side, putting a comforting hand upon her shoulder.

'Sorry there was no time to warn you,' he said kindly. 'But we did tell Doctor Carson about it. He let us have his key so we could put a man inside. You were in no real danger. The Inspector assured you of that.'

'It didn't seem like that to me,' Jane said breathlessly. 'I thought my time had come. Steve said he had poisoned a bottle of whisky. He was going to make me drink some, and take some himself.'

'I heard him say that.' The detective who had been in the lounge came in at the doorway. 'I'm sorry I couldn't let you know I was in the house, Doctor. We thought it would be better if you didn't know.'

'I heard a sound that scared me,' Jane said. 'That's why I left hurriedly, but Steve was waiting outside.'

'If you hadn't turned and dashed back into the house we would have had him with no trouble,' Jim Fraser said. 'We were in a car along the road, and saw him arrive. We were creeping through the garden when you took off, and he followed you inside and locked the door. But you're all right, aren't you?'

'Yes. He didn't hurt me, thanks to you.'

'Well, you'd better get yourself something to drink. You look badly shocked to me. I'm afraid most of this will have to come out at Steve's trial, but it will be better than living in fear that he might show up again and attempt the same sort of thing. Doctor Carson will be here in a moment. Will you be all right until he arrives?'

'There's nothing to be afraid of now Steve is in custody,' Jane said. 'Yes, I'll be all right, Jim.'

'That's the spirit.' He patted her shoulder and turned to leave, pausing to pick up the bottle of whisky that Steve had dropped when he grappled with the detective. He carried it gingerly, for fear of spoiling finger-prints. 'We'll get this checked,' he said. 'If it is poisoned, then you won't have to worry about Steve again for a very long time.'

Left alone, Jane stood irresolute, her heart still beating fast, her nerves ruffled. Poor Steve! She could feel nothing but pity for him. Then she heard footsteps outside, and turned to face the door as it opened. Philip entered, opening his arms to her as he crossed the threshold. She gave a little cry of relief and hurled herself into his embrace. It was only as his strong arms closed about her that the unreality of the moment fled, and she cried in joy as he kissed her. His voice was gentle as he comforted her, and she blurted out the whole story of Steve. By the time she reached the end of her narration she was feeling better.

'You ought to have told me all about it in the first place, Jane,' he gently chided. 'That's what I'm here for in your life. I have to share everything. Anything less than that will make for a poor future.'

Jane agreed, and knew that in the

days ahead she would keep nothing from him. Very soon they would become one in the eyes of the law and in the sight of God. From that moment on she realised that the fairytale had come true!